ARAGON
by
Derrick J. Truesdale

To My Children,
Never let anyone take your fire from you!

Mass cannot be created or destroyed in a closed system; it can only change form.

— The Law of the Conservation of Mass

PROLOGUE

MESOPOTAMIA, 2033 BC

Lightning tore across the dark and rainless sky.

A moment later thunder cracked so hard it seemed to split the Earth.

KRAKOW!

The desert stretched outward like an ancient scar, its dunes rolling low and wide beneath a sky heavy with storm. Though no rain fell, the air was thick with the promise of it, charged, restless, tasting faintly of dust and metal. The land bore the unmistakable weight of the ending of one age and the dawning of another.

Lightning flashed far off on the horizon, silent and distant, illuminating broken stone half-buried in the dunes, the remnants of forgotten walls, toppled columns, the bones of cities which had once believed themselves eternal.

The wind moved steadily, not violently, but with intent, dragging sand across the surface of the earth in long, whispering sheets which hissed like secrets being passed from one era to the next.

The sky churned in layered darkness, deep indigo, bruised violet, and ash-black clouds stacked upon one another without release.

Thunder rolled occasionally, low and distant, never close enough to threaten, but close enough to remind the land that the heavens were awake.

The desert did not resist the storm. It endured it, as it had endured everything else.

The wind came next, violent, dusty, and hot, lifting grit from the banks of the Tigris and throwing it into the man's eyes.

He continued to run anyway.

Bare feet slapped mud and stone as he sprinted along the river, glancing back in anxious bursts. His chest burned. His heart beating like a drum meant for war. caring less about what his physical body would endure but more about the cost expected to be paid

He knew which one of them was angry.

Or rather, he knew it *had* to be one of them.

The others called Soren a demigod. A gifted one. A dangerous one. But Soren hated the title. He didn't kneel to their shrines. He didn't bring sacrifices or burn fat on their altars. He didn't pretend they were the beginning and end of the universe.

He believed his gifts came from God, and that was why they believed he was dangerous.

And that belief, quiet, stubborn, and absolute, had always set him apart from the others.

He tasted dust and whispered a prayer through clenched teeth.

Protect me. Please. Not from the storm...but from them.

Because he had offended his peers.

He had refused them.

And demigods, whatever they called themselves, didn't forgive being denied, especially by one who would be considered an equal.

A shriek tore through the wind.

Soren's blood went cold.

He spotted the cave, low in the earth, half-hidden behind jagged rock. He had found it earlier. He had prayed he wouldn't need it.

Behind him, the sound came again, closer now, followed by the heavy rush of wings.

FALAP.

FALAP.

FALAP.

A giant black dragon broke through the storm, its silhouette blotting out the sky as it dove toward him with a scream which didn't sound like an animal at all.

Soren whirled, raised his hand, and shouted, "PERMEALIS!"

His body shimmered. Turning him translucent.

The dragon slammed to the ground and slid through him like a living shadow, throwing dirt and stone off to the sides.

The dragons' body was vast and black, not merely dark but absent of light, scales absorbing what little illumination the sky offered. Each scale was thick and ancient, edged like forged obsidian, layered with the precision of something built for war rather than flight. When it moved, the sound was not a roar, but the deep, resonant creak of mass and power shifting against itself.

Its wings unfolded slowly, deliberately, enormous, leathery spans that blotted out the stars when lightning flashed behind them.

Veins ran visibly through the membranes, faintly highlighted by the distant storm light, giving the impression of something alive and pulsing with restrained force. When the wings beat the air, the desert answered, sand lifting, dunes reshaping, wind bending to its passage.

The dragon's head was long and angular, crowned with ridged horns that swept back like a crown worn by a god who had never needed permission to exist.

Its eyes burned faintly, not with fire, but with a cold, ancient intelligence, the kind that had watched civilizations form words for fear and then forgotten them. Smoke curled from its nostrils with each slow breath, dissipating quickly in the dry air.

It did not rage. It did not posture.

The dragon simply *was* a living relic of a time when the world had been younger, harsher, and more honest about the price of power.

Soren snapped back into solidity and ran to the creature's head.

The dragon's eyes blinked open, dull with exhaustion, glazed with pain.

"I'm... sorry, Soren," the dragon rasped. "It took everything I had to slow him down... and I still couldn't defeat him."

"Shh," Soren said, voice tight. "Skylar. Save your strength."

Skylar's wings collapsed to his back as he struggled upright, towering even wounded.

Soren turned his head toward the cave.

"We're out of time," he said as he started walking towards the mouth of the cave.

Skylar followed him towards and into the darkness.

Soren touched a wick with his fingertip.

Flame sprang to life.

He then let the wick go and it led them further into the cave.

They moved deeper and deeper until the mouth of the cave vanished behind them and the dark swallowed what little light they carried with them.

"Illuminaris!" Soren commanded.

Small spheres of additional light bloomed along the walls, hovering like patient stars.

Skylar swallowed hard. "Do you mind telling me your plan?"

Soren began humming, low, steady, like a ritual song.

Skylar's voice sharpened. "Soren!"

The humming stopped.

"I'm going to hide you," Soren said. "In a human body."

Skylar took an instinctive step back. "What?"

Soren reached into his satchel and scooped a handful of sand. He sprinkled it over Skylar's head.

"Stop that!" Skylar snapped. "What are you doing?"

"I'm doing what I said."

Skylar's eyes narrowed as he looked at his friend. "The plan was to preserve my bloodline, to keep Petros from becoming a full god."

"It will be preserved," Soren said. "Hidden. Buried in human code."

Skylar's jaw tightened. "If I'm human, if I have human blood, doesn't that give Petros what he wants?"

"No," Soren said firmly. "Petros doesn't want you simply dead. He wants your head with your binares intact, so he can recreate your living flame for his ascension."

Skylar's gaze flickered. "And as a human...?"

"As a human," Soren said, "he can't take what he needs. He won't be able to pull the flame from you the way he can from a dragon."

Soren sprinkled more sand, his hands steady even as the storm outside howled.

"Any descendant you have," he continued, "may carry your hidden bloodline. If the day comes when they must defend themselves, they will be able to shift between, human, dragon, or somewhere in between, with portions of your memory necessary for their survival, intact."

Skylar's breath shook. "My immortality?"

"Reduced," Soren admitted.

"My strength?"

"Decreased."

"My wings?"

Soren looked him in the eye. "Gone...unless the bloodline awakens."

The words hit like a blow.

Skylar turned away, snorted, then faced him again with quiet resignation.

"I trust you my friend," he said. "Do it!"

Soren put more of the sand on Skylar's head and then put his hand on the left side of his face while looking into the left eye of his humongous face.

"Find the sorceress!" demanded Soren.

"Wait...what?" asked Skylar. "Aren't you the sorcerer?"

Soren stepped back and raised his hands.

"That message is for your descendants!"

His voice dropped, reverent and sharp at once.

"By mildest day, through temperate storm... metamoralis the dragon to human form."

The sand on Skylar's head spun, fast, violent, growing into a miniature tornado that wrapped around the dragon's entire body.

For a moment, Skylar vanished behind swirling grit and light.

Then the cyclone shrank, smaller and smaller, until...

...it finally dissipated.

And where the mighty dragon once had been, a naked man now knelt and was shivering.

He had long dark wavy hair. A full black beard. Skin still marked faintly with something that looked like scales if the light struck just right.

Skylar stared at his own hands as if they belonged to someone else.

Soren shoved a bundle of robes at him, and Skylar looked at him wondering where the bundle had come from.

"Put these on. Quickly."

Skylar dressed with shaking fingers.

When he finished, Soren took his hand.

"Come," he said.

They moved to the back wall of the cavern.

Soren waved his palm across the stone.

"Portaralis!"

A black oval split open in the air, an abyss where the world should've been.

But before they stepped through, a sound drifted down the cave passage as the lights behind them started dimming out.

Voices.

Human voices.

Torchlight flickered far behind them.

Soren froze.

Skylar's eyes widened. "Petros?"

Soren's jaw tightened. "He has servants everywhere. Even here."

Footsteps approached, sandaled, hurried, men carrying fire, armed with spears and short blades, shouting into the dark as if the cave itself had offended them.

Skylar's breath caught. "They're..."

"Mortals," Soren said. "And they don't understand what they're hunting."

The torchlight grew brighter. The shadows on the wall stretched.

Soren pulled Skylar toward the portal.

"Now."

They stepped through.

The oval shrank to a pinprick and vanished.

The lights in the cave winked fully out.

A heartbeat later, the torch-bearing men arrived, staring into the darkness with confusion and fear.

"There was something here," one whispered.

"Nothing but wind," another said, voice unsteady. "You were seeing things."

"There's nothing here sire," exclaimed one of the men as another one of the men slowly advanced and noted the wall.

The light from the fire danced off his blue eyes and reflecting his almost jet-black hair color.

"What now Petros?" asked one of the men.

"I smell him...he was here!" growled Petros. "I will find him; he cannot hide from me forever!"

***

Soren and Skylar emerged into noise, human noise.

It was a crowded marketplace. To their left there was loud bargaining. To their right, the smell of sweat and spice and cooked meat

Soren seemed to know exactly where he was going, navigating through the crowd with ease as Skylar followed blindly. Soren then handed a satchel to Skylar.

"This is very important," Soren started, his voice serious. "In the satchel, there is a map of a domicile unit I've procured for you as well as currency for you to obtain some things you will need, food, fresh garments and such."

He paused, looking at Skylar with a mixture of concern and determination. "You will need to obtain a trade, find a wife, start a family for our plan to work successfully!"

Skylar's nerves started to kick in, the weight of his new responsibilities weighing heavily on his shoulders. "What if I am unable to find a partner?" he asked, his voice unsure.

Soren looked at him with a small smile, his blue eyes shining with confidence and accenting his brown even toned skin very well.

Skylar had creamy beige skin and long dark wavy hair. His beard and mustache matched his face perfectly. Skylar was tall for a mortal man, six feet even, and he had a muscular build. His attractiveness was forged without Soren's help, that was all him.

"I don't think that will be a problem," said Soren. "Also, you will still be able to communicate with animals, which may help you with farming or something of that nature, helping ensure you success maintaining and supporting your family."

He then placed his hands on Skylar's shoulders, looking him directly in the eyes. "You can do this my friend!" Sorren assured him. "Petros will be looking for me and may eventually find me and I cannot allow him to find you, so we have to separate. Try not to worry, you are very well hidden, enjoy this new life and know your descendants will always be well suited to defend themselves until Petros can be defeated!"

"Wait," started Skylar, "I have human hands now, can't I just summon Kusanagi and protect myself?"

Soren frowned, "I'm sorry my friend, that is not how she works, but she will one day be called to defend your line."

Skylar's worries started to melt away as he looked at the crowd of humans and then back at his friend, feeling a sense of determination and hope wash over him. "Thank you, my friend," he said with a genuine smile.

Soren stepped back several steps and vanished quickly into the crowd.

And as Skylar turned away, eyeing over the map given him by his friend, he started walking.

Quiet and calm reserve finally broke over Mesopotamia.

1

March 2006
THE STUDENTS AT South Mountain High
School in Arizona were always on the move as
they entered the hallways of the school.

The song *'Jump Around'* by House of Pain
could be heard blasting in the background.

It was March two thousand and four.

With books clutched in their hands and
backpacks slung over their shoulders, the
students hurried to meet up with friends or make
it to class on time.

The energy in the air was deliciously palpable
as everyone eagerly anticipated the day ahead.

As the students filtered into the classrooms,
they were all greeted by the enthusiastic voices of
their teachers, ready to start the day's lessons.

Some students headed straight to their
lockers to grab their textbooks while others
gathered around the bulletin boards, checking for
any important announcements or upcoming
events.

There was a riot of colors and sounds as the
students went about their daily routines.

Amidst the chaos, there was a sense of camaraderie and belonging which permeated the school.

Tyler Landon knelt beside his locker, one knee pressed awkwardly against the cold linoleum, as he bent to retie the loose shoestring on his right sneaker. He'd only noticed it after shutting the locker door, the sharp metallic clang echoing louder than it should have in the hallway. He worked quickly, fingers moving with the practiced urgency of someone who'd learned not to linger too long in exposed positions such as this one.

A bit lanky and shorter than most of the other students crowding the corridor, Tyler had a way of seeming smaller than he already was. Years of being overlooked, or worse, noticed for the wrong reasons, had trained him to fold inward, shoulders slightly hunched, head often dipped as if bracing for impact.

He'd been picked on more times than he cared to count or admit to and usually by people who mistook quiet for weakness and intelligence for something worthy of ridicule.

Black wire-framed non-prescription glasses sat perpetually askew on his face, stark against his pale skin, not magnifying eyes which were always a little too alert, always scanning. His brown hair was fine and uncooperative, cut into an unfortunate bowl shape which framed his face in a way that did him no favors, giving him an unintentional resemblance to a character from a bad comedy, one comparison he'd overheard often enough to never forget.

His clothes didn't help either. Baggy jeans hung loosely from his narrow hips, threatening to slip with every step, and his oversized Metallica T-shirt draped over his thin frame like it belonged to someone else entirely. The shirt was faded from countless washes, the logo cracked and worn, but Tyler wore it anyway, it was one of the few things he liked about himself. Music, at least, didn't judge.

When he finished tying his shoe, he lingered for half a second longer than necessary, taking a breath before standing. The hallway buzzed around him, laughter, lockers slamming, voices overlapping, but Tyler moved through it like a ghost, present and invisible all at once.

He started to walk pass a group of boys taller than him who tripped him, causing him to fall face down as everyone around them laughed.

"Watch where you're going, Land off," laughed Frank, a large, freckled face bully, who turned and faced his friends who all gave him high fives.

"What the fuck Francis?" asked Tyler as he picked himself up off the floor and dusted his pants off. "I'm really impressed you were able to come up with that all by yourself, you know, only being the second generation of your family being able to walk upright and all."

Frank turned and faced Tyler with an angry facial expression as he started shoving him, causing Tyler to stumble back a little.

"You think you're smart you little shit, don't cha?" Frank huffed.

Aaron Gardon turned around after closing his locker and started to watch the confrontation between the two, taking notice of the incredible size differences between Frank and his victim.

"Time out...time out, " started Tyler as he held his hands in a letter 'T' formation. "I just put my jacket in the locker, and you got that thick ass vest jacket on, there's no way this would be a fair fight. You should give your jacket to one of your boys so this fight can be fair."

Frank smiled as he started to take off his vest jacket and turned around smiling as he gave it to one of his friends, "yeah, I'm really gonna enjoy this ass whoop..."

Tyler interrupted Frank by kicking him in the ass and causing Frank to fall forward onto the floor in front of his friends. He then quickly took off.

Aaron laughed. *Pretty smart*, he thought.

Frank got off the floor as some of the kids in the hall, laughed.

"Let's get him!" he demanded as he and his friends took off after Tyler.

Aaron saw the direction the group was headed in and assumed they were headed to the gym. He took off in the direction of a short cut he knew of.

***

Finding a stairwell which only had a few people in it, Tyler quickly dodged those he passed and jumped down a few sets of steps at a time until he got to the basement and started cutting through the gym when he saw another student, Aaron, come in the door from the outside.

Tyler stopped as he looked at him, unsure if the student was with the other group or not. He then heard the door quickly swing open behind him, causing him to turn and look in the direction from where he had come.

"Big mistake Land-off," started Frank as he and the group moved towards him.

"Yo Frank, just chill man," started Aaron from behind Tyler. "You both had your fun, now let it go!"

"Stay out of this Izzy," replied Frank as he threw a hand into his fist and moved towards Tyler.

"Izzy? was that meant to be derogatory?" asked Aaron as he started to move towards Frank, putting himself between Frank and Tyler. "That didn't sound like an endearing vocalization to me."

Frank threw a punch at Tyler, but Aaron caught it.

"Why don't yall try and hit me?" Aaron asked sarcastically.

The small group of boys surrounded Aaron as Tyler moved backwards. They all tried to hit Aaron, but his reflexes proved to be sharp and on point as he blocked or caught each swing or kick coming at him.

Aaron moved like he'd done this before, blocking, stepping, redirecting. Not flashy. Not dramatic. Just efficient.

Tyler stared with awe.

Without any warning, Frank attempted to dart past Aaron towards Tyler, but Aaron caught him in the face, sending the bully flying backwards to the ground.

Frank's friends started to tighten their circle around Aaron.

"ENOUGH!" demanded Principal Stillwater who was headed towards them with two security guards.

Principal Stillwater was a physically fit forty-five-year-old Native American man with a calm, grounded presence which commanded attention without demanding it. He carried himself with disciplined confidence, his posture straight, his expression measured, and his dark eyes observant, missing little, tolerating less.

"All of you, in my office right now!" he demanded.

***

At the end of the school day, Aaron exited out of the main double doors and across the parking lot of the school while observing traffic. He started heading home as the doors of the school opened behind him and Tyler along with a handful of other students exited.

Tyler then started looking around.

After spotting Aaron, Tyler started haphazardly making his way across the lot after him.

"Hey!" he yelled without getting any response. "Yo Aaron! Wait!" he yelled as Aaron kept walking. Tyler quickly caught up to him.

"I wanna thank you," he started, sounding out of breath.

"Yeah well, you need to start picking your battles a little more carefully," replied Aaron.

"Duly noted," replied Tyler. "I'm Tyler by the way," he said, extending his hand.

Aaron looked at Tyler's hand and then at his face. He then continued looking forward as they kept walking.

Aaron was a healthy looking sixteen-year-old. He was physically fit in appearance, had dark brown hair which was somewhat curly at the top. And he dressed in denim pants with a white tee shirt and a denim vest. He wore white Nikes.

"You're not into shaking," started Tyler, "cool!"

"Look," started Aaron, "I'm not really into making friends, I saw something I didn't like, and I got involved!"

"Where'd you learn to fight like that?" Tyler asked excitedly. "That was totally badass!"

"Being Israeli American, my mother has always made sure I knew how to fight," started Aaron, "just in case anyone ever decided to start trouble with me."

Aaron again looked Tyler up and down. "You might wanna take some lessons too!"

Tyler wanted to laugh, but it came out like a little nervous chuckle. "Even if I could fight, look at me. Frank would fold me."

"My grandfather used to always tell me, it's not always about how big someone is, it's about out thinking them. I thought you knew that," added Aaron, "you sure seemed to have kept your wits about you during the confrontation at the lockers."

"Oh, you saw that," started Tyler embarrassed. "I do have a problem keeping quiet when something upsets me...or excites me...it's quite the problem actually."

Tyler then blinked, reflecting on Aaron's words.

"Out thinking your opponent can be so much more impactful than out punching them," added Aaron.

"Well, if there is ever any way I could ever repay you," started Tyler, "don't hesitate to ask...I'm a bit of a techy and could be useful, changing grades, getting you scholarships, yada, yada, yada! My pop works for the government and all!"

Aaron smiled.

"Maybe making a friend isn't the worst thing," he suggested.

Tyler grinned like he'd just won something.

"By the way," started Aaron, "I don't shake hands, I high-five!" Aaron pointed across the street. "I go this way, see you tomorrow?"

"Cool beans," replied Tyler as the two high fived.

Tyler then took off in a different direction.

Aaron then crossed the street and headed a block down from the corner before heading into his home. He walked in the door and dropped his backpack on a bench near the front door.

Aaron's house sat on a quiet residential street. It wasn't large, but it was well kept, orderly, similar in the way homes were when someone inside the home valued control.

The lawn was cut evenly, the walkway swept clean, and the porch light always worked.

Nothing about it called attention to itself, and that seemed intentional.

Inside, the air carried a faint mixture of antiseptic and brewed coffee. The house was tidy but lived in. Furniture was practical rather than unnecessarily decorative; clean lines, neutral tones, surfaces uncluttered except for a few carefully chosen and placed photographs.

One framed picture near the hallway showed Aaron at age six standing between his parents, his father's arm resting proudly on his shoulder.

The frame had been dusted recently.

The kitchen reflected shared responsibilities. A chore list was pinned neatly to the refrigerator, written in precise handwriting.

Dishes were rarely left in the sink for long.

Aaron handled the trash, yard work, and minor repairs while his mother handled appointment scheduling, the bills, and most things that required precision.

There was an unspoken rhythm between them, less spoken affection, more demonstrated loyalty.

Upstairs, Aaron's room contrasted the rest of the house. It was orderly but personal.

Books were stacked near his desk; a lamp was angled just right for late night study sessions. There was a modest full-sized bed, neatly made. Nothing flashy. Nothing careless.

His mother's presence was felt even when she wasn't home. Her medical journals sometimes rested on the dining table; surgical textbooks were marked with tabs.

Her work demanded steadiness, and that steadiness carried into the house.

She was protective in subtle ways, double-checking locks at night, asking more questions than necessary, watching Aaron a second longer before leaving for a shift, day or night.

Their home felt safe. It was structured. It was also a little guarded.

Like the two of them.

"Mom, I'm home!" yelled Aaron.

He received no response.

He then headed into the kitchen and found a note on the refrigerator door.

Ha, knew you would see this, had to go in for an emergency surgery, dinner's in the microwave, Love mom!

"Of course," laughed Aaron, "love you too mom!"

2

NAPLES, ITALY.

The sky hung low and bruised over the Bay of Naples, thick clouds swallowing the last traces of twilight. A cold, wet wind rolled in off the Tyrrhenian Sea, carrying with it the sharp scent of salt and stone. It was the kind of damp chill that didn't merely touch the skin, it crept through fabric, through muscle, until it seemed to settle in the marrow.

The narrow streets glistened beneath scattered lamplight, centuries-old cobblestones slick with mist. Laundry lines swayed faintly between faded buildings, the shutters rattling as gusts of wind funneled through the tight corridors of the city.

Somewhere in the distance, a church bell tolled, its hollow echo swallowed by the restless surf crashing against the seawall.

Alessio Adregoni continued to run anyway.

He tore through the winding streets toward Castel dell'Ovo, lungs burning, shoes slapping against ancient stone polished smooth by generations long dead.

His breath came in ragged bursts, vanishing instantly into the cold air.

The fortress loomed ahead on the small island of Megaride, its dark silhouette rising from the water like something older than memory itself.

He didn't look back.

He didn't want to look back.

Not until he had to.

Not until the sensation struck him, sharp and deliberate, like a blade pressed lightly against the base of his spine.

He was being hunted.

Not by police.

Not by criminals.

By something older.

And he feared for his life.

He reached the castle wall and leapt.

Not a struggle. Not a climb.

A jump which should've been impossible, up to the first ledge, then the next.

His skin rippled, briefly shifting into a scaly texture before smoothing out again.

The man's skin then fully converted to a green scaly like structure as his eyes began to look more reptilian.

He ran along the length of the wall and then jumped up again, making it to the top and then a growth spurt of about two feet.

As the two men running after him soon reached the wall, they also soon leapt up with no effort, following their quarry to the top of the famous tourist attraction.

As the reptilian looking man turned backwards and slowly, steadily kept backing away from his would-be assailants, the sudden appearance of a third man, strangely dressed in an Armani suit, startled him.

"Alessio Adregoni!" started Petros as he followed his cronies to the rightfully frightened man. "Your forefathers erroneously thought that changing a few letters around in your sur name was going to hide you from me. Now here we are, and I am moments from achieving my ascension!"

"Go to Hell!" demanded an angry Alessio.

Petros chuckled as he peered behind the dragon / man hybrid, "so original Alessio! It seems you have no wings and cannot take flight, so I'll be sending you there first!"

Alessio turned and looked behind himself, studying a path to the large body of water. *If I am unable to make the swim,* he thought, *at least he won't be able to get what he came for.* He quickly turned and ran for the edge of the castle wall and dove out and into the large body of water.

Petros stopped in his tracks as his two henchmen just turned and looked back at him. Petros shook his head in the negative and then pointed at the body of water where Alessio went in, raised his hand up and swirled them together as if he were mixing something, and then raised his right hand up and back as if he were a fisherman who just casted a line and was bringing in his catch.

A soaking wet and coughing Alessio came flying backwards out of the water until he landed in front of Petros as a sword shimmered into existence in the demi-God's hand.

Alessio looked up angrily at Petros while coughing, expelling excess water from within. "No matter what you do... you will never be a true God!"

Petros held up the sword, preparing to decapitate his victim. "I would show you that you are wrong, but you will never live to see it anyway!" He then quickly swung the sword down and took Alessio's head clean off dropping his sword and raising his arms up.

He stood by as if he were waiting for something to happen.

Nothing happened.

"Maybe you need to light the flames closer to Mount Vesuvius?" suggested one of the henchmen.

Petros lowered his arms. "No," he started, "igniting the dragon flames shouldn't have been a problem, I should have started my ascension here and now!" He picked up the half human and half dragon head.

"He wasn't the last one." He then dropped the head onto the roof top. "Let's go, we've got work to do."

***

Aaron jumped up suddenly, sweat all over his body, breathing hard and fast as if something were wrong as he reached for his head and neck while tears streamed down his cheeks.

He sat in his bed and looked around his dark room, noticing the time at three seventeen a. m.

His breathing slowly started to normalize, respirations and heart rate both slowly decreasing.

As he looked around his room, he couldn't help but to think about how he could see everything clearly, even as dark as it currently was with all of the lights out.

He removed his blanket and then turned to sit on the left side of his bed, still taking the time to calm himself, still wondering why he awoke the way he had. Then he heard a voice in his head.

Find the sorceress!

"Who said that?" he asked nervously as he quickly turned around.

Nothing.

"Get a grip Aaron," he said out loud and to himself.

He soon stood up and headed to the bathroom and as he walked in, he swore his eyes looked almost animal like for a brief moment startling himself, but then upon a second quick glance, his eyes were normal.

He stared in the mirror for a minute longer and then turned the faucet on. He splashed some cold water on his face.

Being respectful of his mother, Aaron closed the bathroom door before relieving himself. He then flushed the toilet, washed his hands and headed back to bed.

As soon as he laid down.

Find the sorceress!

He heard it again and quickly jumped up again.

"What the hell?" he asked frightened.

Find the sorceress!

Find the sorceress!

"MOM!" he yelled as he covered his ears.

A few moments later, Aaron's mother came running into the room wearing baggy shorts and a tee shirt. She turned his lamp on and then sat on the bed and hugged him as he sat there holding his ears. "Aaron, what's wrong?"

Aaron then thought about how much his mother already seemed to worry about him.

"Just a bad dream," he lied. "I'm sorry I woke you."

"It's okay," I wasn't fully asleep anyway. "Are you sure you're okay?"

"If I'm not, I will be," he replied.

She kissed him on the forehead. "Okay, try to get a little more sleep, you have a few hours before you have to be in school."

"Yup," he said as he laid down and watched her turn the light off.

His mother soon left out of the room.

As he looked around his darkened room, he closed his eyes.

Find the sorceress!

3

SOMEWHAT DISTRACTED BY the events of the previous night, Aaron sleepily put some books in his locker while grabbing other books out. He appeared to really be just going through the motions when he suddenly closed his locker and found Tyler standing there grinning.

"Buenos dias! mi nuevo capadre!" greeted Tyler.

"I'm not Spanish," replied Aaron as he started walking off with Tyler trailing him.

Tyler laughed. "I know that my friend, I just have Spanish next and I always take every opportunity to get practice in before a test." He then looked at Aaron's face. "Man you look like shit! Are you okay?"

"Rough night," replied Aaron while sleepily yawning without stopping. He then stopped in front of a classroom door and turned and looked at Tyler.

"I don't..." he paused as he gripped the doorknob to his classroom and opened it.

Another student quickly walked in.

"Do you think you can meet me after school?" Aaron asked. "I have a problem and I think I need to talk to someone before I bust."

Find the sorceress!

Aaron jumped. "You hear that?"

Tyler looked at Aaron as if he discovered his new friend might be on drugs. "Yeah, you asked if I could meet you after school. Where, the front?"

Aaron sighed. "Yeah, see you then." he then entered and closed the door.

Tyler just shrugged as he walked off.

***

After school, many of the teenagers spilled out and darted off in various directions as Tyler stood casually leaning back against the building wall near the entrance, awaiting his new friend.

He soon spied Aaron heading out with his red and white school jacket on and his backpack situated over his back.

"YO AARON!" he called.

Aaron spotted him and headed in his direction.

"So what was it you wanted to talk about?" asked Tyler as the pair just started walking.

"Do you have time to kill?" Aaron asked. "This shit has been bugging me all day."

"Look Out Point," suggested Tyler, "we can walk there in like fifteen minutes, no one usually heads there until about sundown."

"Perfect," said Aaron as the two started walking. "I can explain part of it on the way."

"I'm all ears," Tyler said smiling.

"Well, you said you're good at researching stuff, and I need to know that what I tell you and ask of you stays between you and I!"

"You better not ask me about no freaky shit," started Tyler. "I know we cool but I just got off punishment!"

"No," argued Aaron, "nothing like that!"

"Well good because...I know I'm cute and all, but this booty hole is a one-way street."

Aaron gave him the side eye. "What's wrong with you?"

"My bad dude," corrected Tyler. "What's up?"

"Can you keep this between us?"

"Yeah dude, sure."

"For the past two weeks," started Aaron as they turned up a path and headed up to look out point. "I've been having these dreams. It's like me, but I'm someone else, if that makes sense?"

"You're dreaming as if you are the character, but the character is actually someone else! Got it"

"The dreams...they're always in different locations, and I am always someone different, but the outcome is always the same."

"And that is?"

"I get my head sliced off by this weird looking model dude with a ponytail!"

"That is some freaky shit dude, you get your head sliced off every time?"

"Every time!"

"Here's the even stranger part," started Aaron. "One time, as the head was falling, I could see the reflection of the fallen head and..."

He paused as he thought about how silly it would sound. "I would see... the face of some sort of reptile...almost dragon-like."

"What...no way!" exclaimed Tyler laughingly.

"Way," replied Aaron. "And then there is a voice that keeps repeating in the dream as well as while I'm awake."

"What does the voice say?" asked Tyler.

Aaron stared at Tyler. "Find the sorceress,"
his last word changed into a growl as his face
metamorphosized into that of a hybrid-
man/dragon.

Tyler screamed the high-pitched wail of a
little girl as he started running while turning back
and keeping his eyes on Aaron.

Not realizing why Tyler was so scared Aaron
reached out towards him and with a deep voice
said, "Tyler wait!" He then looked at his hands
and saw leathery looking scales. "What the hell?"

Tyler kept walking backwards while keeping
his eye on Aaron.

Tyler stepped back without looking, and his
heel hit empty air.

Tyler's scream tore out of him as he fell
backwards off the cliff.

"TYLER!" without a thought Aaron ran to the
edge and dove off after him, immediately
catching up to his crying friend.

And then something ripped open behind
Aaron's shoulders.

Sounds of tearing cloth.

Wings, huge, leathery, real, burst through his
jacket.

The wings opened wide like bilateral chutes,
FALAP, slowing their descent, but as if on
instinct, Aaron flapped again and they quickly
moved upwards.

FALAP.

FALAP.

They shot back toward the cliff in a single
violent swoop.

As soon as he let Tyler go, Aaron landed a few feet ahead of him and stumbled a bit as his wings retracted into his back and the scales started to fade away, returning his features to normal.

Aaron tore the rest of his jacket off and looked at the large slits in the back where the wings had come through. His tee shirt had large rips in them as well.

"WHAT THE HELL WAS THAT?" yelled Tyler. "You brought me up here to pull some elaborate punk type shit on me?"

Aaron quickly doubled over to catch his breath, not because he couldn't breathe but because he was having a panic attack.

"AARON, can you hear me?"

Aaron tried to speak.

The last thing he saw was Tyler's silently screaming mouth and terrified face.

Aaron then blacked out and fell over.

***

Over in Italy, a surge of adrenaline coursed through Petros' veins as he made his way through the winding corridors of the ancient castle. He had been searching for years, scouring every corner of the world for the source of supernatural power which had eluded him for so long.

Finally, he had found it, and this time, he wouldn't let it slip through his fingers.

Bursting into the lower-level activity hall, Petros interrupted his two henchmen in the midst of a game of pool.

"Pack your bags."

The cue ball cracked into motion. Balls scattered across green felt.

32

Both men turned.

Petros stood near the entrance, hands folded behind his back, eyes bright with something close to satisfaction.

Cage straightened. "That was fast."

Byron squinted. "You found another one?"

Petros smiled, not wide, not dramatic. Just enough.

"Not just another one," he said. "The strongest I've sensed in centuries."

Byron let out a low whistle. "Where?"

"America."

Cage snapped his fingers. "America? Then why don't you just..." he mimed an explosion with his hands. "...poof us over there?"

Petros's smile faded.

"That kind of carelessness and those types of actions are how hidden bloodlines disappear," he said calmly. "Not how they're harvested."

He walked around the pool table, fingertips brushing the edge as if he were inspecting a chessboard.

"When dragon blood awakens," he continued, "it resonates. It calls. If I answer that call with too much magic, he will feel me."

Byron frowned. "He? You sure?"

Petros stopped walking.

"Yes."

He looked down at the table, at the scattered balls, solids and stripes intermingled without order.

"The bloodline has mostly favored males," Petros said. "And over the years I've been able to tell them apart..."

He exhaled slowly.

"This one is loud."

Cage leaned against the table. "So what's the plan, boss?"

"We move like humans," Petros said. "Flights. we follow paper trails. we will do surveillance. We check out the schools, this one's young. and we be mindful of where the hospitals are in case, we only hurt him and he manages to get away."

His eyes darkened with memory.

"I've waited centuries. I can wait a few more days."

Byron sank the eight-ball with a clean shot.

Petros didn't look at the table.

"Once he understands what he is," Petros said quietly, "he'll start looking for answers."

He turned toward the door.

"And when he does... I'll be there to give them to him."

4

"AARON!" YELLED TYLER while smacking Aaron in the face as the sky started to darken.

Tyler then raised his hand up one more time and hesitated for a brief second before bringing his hand down to Aaron's face.

Aaron quickly caught Tyler's hand, just before it reached his face as he opened his eyes.

"If you ever slap me again..."

"What the hell was that?" interrupted Tyler as Aaron started sitting up. "You looked like..."

"A half man half dragon?" asked Aaron.

"How did this happen?"

"I don't know," started Aaron as they both stood fully up, "but this must be related to my dreams."

"You think?" Tyler asked sarcastically.

"Okay...think...Aaron...think," started Aaron as he started anxiously pacing back and forth while Tyler briefly marveled at his ripped shirt. "This all means something, the dreams, the strange man killing people who look like dragons..."

"FIND THE SORCERESS!!" they both exclaimed simultaneously.

Aaron put his hands on Tyler's shoulders startling him a bit.

"Like I started to say Tyler, I could really use
your help!"

"We can go to my house," Tyler said
anxiously.

***

As Tyler and Aaron made their way to Tyler's
house, they couldn't help but discuss the bizarre
events experienced in the past couple of hours.

Aaron texted his mother to let her know
where he would be.

With Tyler he then shared his theories about
the significance of his dreams and the mysterious
figure with the ponytail.

Tyler, being the good friend that he was
trying to be, remained optimistic and assured
Aaron they would get to the bottom of everything.

After arriving at Tyler's house, Aaron's eyes lit
up with awe as he stepped into the basement. It
was a tech enthusiast's dream, with the latest
gadgets and computer setups.

Tyler proudly showed off his creations,
explaining each one with excitement.

Aaron was impressed, seeing the room filled
with innovative contraptions and gadgets,
knowing that Tyler's skills would come in handy
one day.

"This is incredible!" he exclaimed, taking it all
in.

"This is where I do my research," Tyler
explained while beaming with pride. "I even have
processors from Microsoft not meant for the
public until at least two thousand and five."

"One year isn't really that big of a difference,"
started Aaron, sounding unimpressed.

Tyler beamed at Aaron. "It is if you want to stay ahead on the information superhighway!"

Aaron felt a surge of hope, knowing with Tyler's resources and his own determination, they might just stand a chance at unraveling the enigma haunting his dreams before something bad happened to him.

Tyler sat down at his computer and started it up. "Grab a chair," he said as he gestured to the other side of the room towards another chair. "Whatever you do, just don't go breathing fire on anything."

Aaron laughed. "I can't breathe fire!"

"Did you know when you woke up this morning your skin could get scaly or you could fly?"

Aaron stopped smiling and while Tyler was focused on the computer screen, he held his hand up to his face and blew on it.

"I was serious when said don't breathe fire in here," said Tyler without turning around.

Aaron looked at the computer. "What are you doing?"

"I'm doing a keyword search to see if I can get us any information," Tyler replied as he typed in the word 'dragon'.

"You really think you'll find anything on the misinformation superhighway?" asked Aaron.

"What? You have something against technology?" Tyler answered the question with another question. "Remember...you came to me and asked me for my help."

"I have a cell phone," started Aaron as he held up his flip phone, "that's about as techy as I get."

"Dragon speaking naturally...," started Tyler in a voice so low, it seemed as if he were talking to himself. "Yadda, yadda, yadda...so most of the information I am finding on dragons or anything dragon related is dictation software, fantasy related, myths and the like," said Tyler.

Tyler turned and faced Aaron briefly. "The legends of them started in Mesopotamia...like two thousand years B - C."

"That's something," started Aaron hopefully, "My family is from Israel...my dad much more recent than my mom."

"Well, there's not much there for us to go on," said Tyler. "Wait, did your dad ever tell you about any of this?"

"My dad died when I was young, very young," replied Aaron.

"Hmm," started Tyler, "Hey check this out!"

"What?" replied Aaron as he looked at the screen.

"Anagrams for the word dragon," laughed Tyler, "Your name is up there."

"Get out of here," started Aaron, "there aren't enough letters in Aaron to spell the word dragon."

"Not your first name lizard breath," chuckled Tyler, "Gardon, your last name."

Aaron thought that was strange. "Coincidence!" he argued.

"Well I'm going with it," replied Tyler. "We should come up with an anagram of your full name to come up with your superhero name."

Aaron laughed. "Superhero name? I just want to save my ass, so that I'm not decapitated."

"Organon, Roanna!" exclaimed Tyler.

"I'm not doin' this."

"Aaron, no that's already your name," realized Tyler. "How about Dana?"

"That's a girls name!"

"Works for Jade, and he's in Philly!"

"Tyler!"

"I know, Gonad!"

"Tyler!"

"Aragon!"

"TYLER!" Aaron yelled causing Tyler to turn and face him.

"I think my life is at stake here," started Aaron tiredly, "please focus!"

"Okay, okay," replied Tyler as he sighed and turned and faced the computer again. "Lets' try another search phrase. "Find the sorceress," he said as he typed on the keyboard.

"I'm sorry," started Aaron as he got up and started pacing around the basement. "I'm just scared for my life."

Aaron then stared hard at the computer.

"I get it," said Tyler right before he started mumbling to himself as he read some of the items that came up on his computer screen.

"Shit," he started, "here's something!" Tyler started pointing at the screen so Aaron could follow along. "In nineteen thirty-five, an Israeli man living in Italy took his own life after seeking help from authorities, ranting on about dreams he was having of a long-haired man trying to kill him so that his dragon blood line would cease to exist."

"That sounds like my problem," interjected Aaron.

"The man claimed," continued Tyler, "to give up hope after having a hard time finding a sorceress. Many dismissed his claims as nonsense and the man, his wife, and unborn child were never found. The man's younger brother who was believed to have left the country, was never heard from again either."

"It seems like finding this sorceress will be my only hope," sighed Aaron, "I didn't even know I was part dragon until today." Aaron turned and plopped down in his chair as Tyler stared hard at the computer screen as if he were reading something else.

Tyler chuckled.

"You are really going to appreciate my love for word puzzles," started Tyler as Aaron rolled the chair over towards Tyler and looked at the screen.

On the screen, *Sor_cerhess777 located on Facebook*.

"What is Facebook?"

"Its a social platform for college students," replied Tyler.

"Just college students?" asked Aaron.

"Yup," started Tyler. "Well, for now anyway, I think everyone will have it one day."

"It can't be that easy," started Aaron.

"What? Hiding in plain sight?" asked Tyler. "We'll find out soon enough." He started typing on the keyboard.

"What are you doing?" asked Aaron.

"Sending her a friend request and a little message."

"But you don't go to college...how do you have a Facebook account?"

"Didn't I say I was a tech wiz?"

5

THE MALL FELT too bright.

Not because it was different than any other afternoon at Desert Ridge, sun exposed spots, fluorescent lights, polished tile, the smell of pretzels and cinnamon, but because Aaron's senses wouldn't settle everything landed sharp.

Every sound seemed separated into pieces: shoes squeaking, a baby crying, somebody laughing near the food court like it was the easiest thing in the world.

Tyler walked half a step behind him, trying to act normal, which meant he was talking too much.

"So listen," Tyler said, hands in his pockets, eyes sweeping the crowd as if he was half proud while also being half terrified to be part of something dangerous. "This is either the beginning of our origin story... or we're about to get murdered near a Foot Locker."

Aaron didn't laugh.

His phone buzzed again and he looked at the screen.

There was no caller ID.

There was no telephone number.

Just a message which had come through the same way the Facebook account had on Tyler's computer, like it didn't care what rules normal communication followed.

Meet me somewhere public. Mall, Desert Ridge. Don't bring attention to yourself. Do not go alone.

Aaron stared at the screen until the words blurred.

"She text you again?" Tyler asked.

Aaron nodded.

Tyler's grin faltered. "You think she's real?"

"I think..." Aaron began, then stopped.

He didn't want to say *I hope so* out loud. Hope felt like a dare right now.

"I think I'll be optimistic," he finally said in a low tone.

They turned a corner near a kiosk selling phone cases and cheap jewelry.

Two teenage girls leaned over a display of glittery earrings, squealing like they had no idea the world could be anything else but soft and simple.

Aaron envied them for a second.

Then his wrist got a tingling sensation under his sleeve.

Not quite an itch.

Not a burning sensation.

Just that sensation you get when you can feel someone staring at the side of your head.

Aaron slowed.

Tyler bumped into him. "Yo, what's wrong?"

Aaron's eyes scanned the open corridor.

At first, nothing stood out.

Aaron only noticed shoppers, strollers, and couples holding hands. He then saw a security guard yawning near the entrance of a department store.

Then Aaron saw someone else.

A man near the pretzel place, tall, broad, wearing a neutral jacket, standing as if he was waiting for someone. His face was ordinary enough that Aaron almost looked away.

But his posture wasn't, like he was looking for something.

Too still. Too ready.

And when the man turned his head, his eyes met Aaron's from across the crowd.

Aaron's throat tightened.

The man didn't smile like a normal person.

He smiled like someone who recognized property.

Tyler's voice dropped. "Aaron…"

"You see him?" Aaron whispered.

"Yeah," Tyler said. "And I don't like how my stomach just did a backflip."

Aaron grabbed Tyler by the elbow, not hard, just enough to pull him into motion.

"Walk this way," Aaron said. "Don't run."

Tyler swallowed. "We're leaving? Like now?"

"Now!"

They moved through the crowd at a fast walk. Aaron forced himself not to look back. Forced his breath to stay even. Forced his steps to match the pace of normal people.

But his heartbeat didn't listen.

They passed the food court.

They passed the movie theater.

Aaron pushed through the double doors into the dry Arizona heat, sunlight slamming into them like a wall.

Outside, the parking lot shimmered, and the sky was cruelly blue.

"Okay," Tyler said, voice shaking now that they were outside. "Now we can run, right?"

Aaron finally looked back through the glass doors, his vision extra keen, zoomed all the way to where the man was standing.

The man was still inside.

Still calm.

Still watching.

But now he wasn't alone.

A second figure stood a few feet behind him, leaner, hands in his pockets, moving with the same wrong stillness.

Two.

Aaron's skin tightened.

"Is he not following?" Tyler asked.

"Oh they're following," Aaron said. "They're just doing it like they got all day."

"They?" Tyler cursed under his breath. "Whatta we do?"

Aaron's eyes flicked to the edge of the parking lot, past the last row of cars, where the city broke into dust and scrub and the flat wild stretch beyond.

His chest pulled that way.

Not logic, but instinct.

"The desert," Aaron said.

Tyler stared at him. "Are you serious? Why would we go *toward* the desert?"

Aaron didn't have time to explain the feeling in his bones, like some part of him remembered the sand.

"Trust me," Aaron said angrily, and he then realized that came out harsher than he meant for it to. "Just trust me," he repeated calmly.

Tyler nodded once. "Okay. Okay. I'm trusting you. But if I die in a cactus field, I'm haunting you."

Aaron broke into a run.

Tyler ran with him.

They cut between rows of parked cars, hopped a low barrier, and the paved world gave way to dirt and rocks and brittle weeds.

Heat rose off the ground in waves, dry enough to crack your throat with each breath.

Behind them, the mall sat quiet and normal, as if it had nothing to do with anything.

Aaron ran harder.

Tyler wheezed. "You...are you sure...this is the play?"

Aaron's answer was a growl.

Not the kind he made on purpose. His fingers tingled. His nails sharpened just slightly, thickening into something darker.

"No," Aaron said, voice tightening. "I'm not sure of anything."

He felt it again.

That pressure behind his eyes. That buzzing in his ears.

The voice had been silent since his first metamorphosis. But its absence didn't comfort him. It felt like the air right before a lightning strike.

They crested a small ridge of sandstone and dropped down into a shallow slope which led to a natural opening in the earth, part cave, part erosion cut, hidden by brush and shadow.

Aaron stopped.

Tyler almost ran into him. "What, what is this?"

"A way out," Aaron said.

"A way out of what? Life?"

Aaron stepped into the mouth of the cave.

Cool air washed over him immediately, damp and mineral scented.

The sunlight behind them dimmed, replaced by shadows and the faint echo of their own breathing.

Tyler hesitated, then followed. "Bro, if there's bats in here..."

"There won't be," Aaron said, though he didn't know how he knew.

The tunnel widened, then split.

The rock walls looked like honeycomb with natural pockets and holes carved by time. There were little chambers branching off as if they were secret passageways.

Tyler's voice softened. "This is insane."

Aaron kept moving.

He didn't know where he was going, only that his body did.

And then the air changed.

Not temperature.

Intent.

Aaron stopped so hard Tyler bumped him again.

Tyler muttered, "For the love of..."

Aaron lifted a hand.

Tyler went quiet.

Ahead, in the shadow where the tunnel opened into a wider chamber, two figures stood as if they had been waiting for them the entire time.

The first was broad-shouldered, heavy in the chest, wearing dark clothes which didn't belong out here. His head was shaved. His arms looked like they had never known softness.

The second was leaner, with a narrow face and a calm expression which didn't match the situation. He stood slightly behind the big one, hands relaxed at his sides.

Neither one looked winded.

Neither one looked surprised.

The big one spoke first, voice low and amused.

"You run funny," he said.

Tyler's breath hitched. "Aaron…"

Aaron's heart hammered.

He didn't know these men.

But he knew what they were.

Not because of scales or claws or glowing eyes.

Because the space around them felt wrong, like the cave itself didn't want them inside it.

Aaron stepped forward, shoulders tight. "What do you want?"

The lean man tilted his head, studying Aaron like a specimen. "What do you think?"

The big one cracked his knuckles. "We want you!"

Tyler took a step back. "We didn't do anything."

The big one's eyes flicked to Tyler, just once, dismissive. "You don't matter."

Aaron felt something in his chest snap.

His skin prickled. Heat surged up his spine.

"Don't talk to him," Aaron said, voice deepening. "Talk to me."

The lean man smiled slightly. "That's the idea."

The big one moved first.

He crossed the distance too fast to be human.

Aaron barely had time to react before a fist came at him like a wrecking ball.

Aaron ducked, the punch slicing air inches above his head, and he then slammed his shoulder into the man's ribs.

It should've hurt the man.

It didn't.

It felt like hitting a wall.

Aaron staggered back, blinking.

Tyler shouted, "What the hell!"

The lean man moved now, not rushing, just stepping in at an angle and throwing something small.

A flash of cold pain burned across Aaron's side.

Aaron looked down.

A thin cut had appeared on his shirt, blood wetting the fabric.

Aaron's mouth went dry.

He hadn't even seen the weapon.

The big one laughed. "There you go. Bleed a little for us."

Aaron backed up angrily, breath ragged. His fingers curled, nails thickening again into something darker.

His eyes stung.

Something pressed behind them.

Tyler's voice shook. "Aaron, what do we do?"

Aaron's jaw tightened. "We don't die."

He lunged.

This time, his body didn't move like it used to.

It moved like it was remembering something older.

He swung fast at the big one, and for a split second, his hand wasn't fully human it was more reptilian-like, his knuckles were ridged, his fingers slightly longer, strength surging into the strike.

The punch landed.

The big one's head snapped to the side with a loud crack.

He grunted, surprised.

Tyler let out a half laugh of disbelief. "Oh! Okay! Okay!"

The lean man's eyes sharpened.

"He can't control it yet," he said quietly.

Aaron didn't know what that meant, but he hated how the man sounded pleased.

The big one turned his head to face Aaron as the sound of cracking bone sounded, as if his neck repaired itself. The big man then charged again, and Aaron dodged, faster now. Not faster than a car, but faster than he should be able to move at all.

He darted sideways, grabbed Tyler's shirt, and yanked him out of the path of the incoming blow.

Tyler stumbled. "Bro!"

"I got you," Aaron snapped, and didn't know if he was talking to Tyler or himself.

The big one then slammed a fist into the rock wall where Tyler had been. The stone cracked.

Dust rained down from the crack.

Tyler screamed. "WHAT ARE YOU PEOPLE?!"

The lean man's expression didn't change. "Hungry."

Aaron's blood went cold.

He backed toward another tunnel branching off the chamber. His eyes flicked around, searching.

There.

A narrow opening higher up the rock, like a vertical crack.

Aaron's shoulders tensed.

He didn't have a plan.

But he had wings.

He didn't know why that thought came with certainty. He only knew it did.

Aaron grabbed Tyler's wrist. "Run when I say run."

Tyler's eyes were wide. "I have been running since you turned into a reptile on a cliff."

"Tyler."

Tyler shut up.

The big one surged forward again.

Aaron waited until the last possible second. "NOW!"

Aaron shoved Tyler toward the tunnel, then turned and jumped, straight up.

His back burned.

Not pain.

Pressure.

Then—

With a violent rip, something tore free.

Two massive leathery wings erupted from Aaron's shoulder blades, unfurling in the tight cavern with a sound like sails catching wind.

Tyler screamed again, higher pitched than the first time. "OH MY GOD!"

Aaron didn't have time to be embarrassed.

FALAP. He beat his wings once.

The air thundered.

FALAP.

He grabbed Tyler by the back of his shirt and yanked him off the ground as he launched toward the upper crack.

Tyler flailed. "I HATE THIS! I HATE ALL OF THIS!"

Aaron's wing brushed the rock wall, sparks of dust flying. He grimaced, adjusted, and squeezed into the crack like a dart.

They burst into a narrow tunnel above the chamber.

Aaron landed hard, sliding, wings scraping.

Tyler hit the ground and rolled, coughing. "I think my soul left my body."

Aaron's wings folded instinctively, fitting tight to his back like they belonged there.

He grabbed Tyler again. "Move."

They ran.

The tunnels twisted, honeycomb pockets opening into dead ends, forcing them to double back. Aaron's lungs burned, but not from exhaustion, more like his body was fighting to stay human while everything else begged to become something else.

Behind them, footsteps echoed.

Steady.

Not rushed.

Tyler's voice cracked. "How are they still behind us?"

Aaron glanced back.

The lean man appeared at the mouth of a tunnel like he had stepped out of the shadow itself.

No heavy breathing.

No anger.

Just patience.

Aaron's stomach dropped.

The big one followed seconds later, grinning.

"You can fly," the big one said. "That's cute."

Aaron's throat tightened. "Leave us alone!"

The lean man's eyes narrowed slightly. "That isn't how this ends."

Aaron pushed Tyler ahead, then turned, claws flashing again at his fingertips.

"I'm not letting you touch him," Aaron growled.

The big one took a step forward.

The lean man lifted a hand, not a dramatic gesture, just an idle motion like a conductor.

Aaron froze.

Not because he chose to.

Because something invisible gripped him from the inside.

Tyler's voice rose in panic. "Aaron?!"

Aaron tried to speak.

Nothing came out but a strained sound.

His skin crawled.

His cheekbones pulled.

His teeth felt like they were rearranging like they were trying to become something else.

Aaron staggered, hands flying to his face.

He felt something happening.

He felt his mouth pushing forward.

He felt the wrong shape trying to claim him.

"Aaron...bro...fight it!"

Aaron's eyes watered.

He shook his head violently, trying to break the invisible hold, trying to keep his face his own.

The pressure increased.

Aaron's vision doubled.

He tasted iron.

Then...

It faltered.

For a second, the force slipped like a hand losing grip on wet stone.

Aaron gasped, collapsing to one knee.

Cage looked at his hand. "Why isn't this working? The boss said it would work!"

His face snapped back, human, trembling, sweating.

The lean man blinked.

It was the first sign of surprise he had shown.

"Interesting," Byron murmured.

Cage frowned. "What happened?"

The big man didn't answer. His eyes scanned the tunnel around them, as if listening for something he couldn't hear.

Aaron lifted his head slowly, shaking.

Tyler crouched beside him, whispering, "What the hell was that? He was… making you…"

"I don't know," Aaron rasped. "But I felt it."

The lean man took a step forward again.

"Get up," he said calmly.

Tyler snapped, voice shaking with rage. "Back the hell up!"

The big one laughed. "The little humans' got a mouth."

Aaron forced himself to stand, wings twitching behind him.

His instincts screamed: *fly.*

But there wasn't enough space.

Not here.

He backed up, putting himself between Tyler and them.

The lean man's gaze lingered on Aaron's torn shirt where the wings once were. "You're ready," he said, almost conversational. "Just not quite there yet."

Aaron swallowed. "I don't even know what that's supposed to mean."

The lean man's mouth curved. "You will, but by then it'll be too late."

The pressure returned all at once.

Not gradual. Not testing.

Aaron screamed as he grabbed the sides of his head.

His body then jerked violently as something seized him by the throat and yanked him off the ground.

Not the lean man this time.

He gasped, feet kicking uselessly as the tunnel floor dropped away beneath him.

Tyler screamed, "AARON!"

Aaron clawed at his own neck, but there was no hand there, nothing physical to grab. Still, he was held, suspended, the air crushed out of his lungs as if the cave itself had decided to strangle him.

Then Petros stepped forward from out of nowhere.

Not hurried. Not angry.

Just...inevitable.

He moved past his henchmen as though they were furniture, his presence bending the space around him in a way Aaron couldn't understand.

Tall, composed, eyes ancient and unreadable, Petros studied Aaron like a craftsman examining flawed material.

"So," Petros said calmly, "this is all that remains of Skylar's bloodline?"

Aaron's vision swam.

His wings twitched at the tip of his back spasming uselessly as his body fought the invisible grip.

Tyler rushed forward instinctively.

One of the henchmen blocked him with a single arm, shoving him back against the rock wall.

"Stop!" Tyler yelled, voice breaking. "You're killing him!"

Petros didn't look at Tyler.

"Not yet," he said. "If I wanted him dead, this would already be finished."

Petros raised one hand slightly.

Aaron's body lifted higher, his neck craning back painfully as his toes dangled inches above the stone.

Petros stepped closer until they were eye level.

"You feel it, don't you?" Petros said softly. "The pressure. The memory. The shape you're supposed to wear."

Aaron's face burned.

Not metaphorically.

Physically.

His jaw tightened, bones aching as something *pushed* from the inside, trying to stretch, to elongate, to become what Petros demanded.

Aaron choked, eyes watering.

"I...can't..." he rasped.

Petros tilted his head, mildly curious.

"You can," Petros corrected him. "You simply won't."

Aaron's teeth ground together as the pressure intensified.

His cheekbones pulled. His gums screaming in pain from his resistance. His vision fractured.

For a terrifying second, Tyler saw it, Aaron's face *almost* slipping, skin rippling like it didn't know what shape it wanted to be.

Tyler shouted, "STOP IT!"

Petros's voice remained calm, almost instructional.

"Bring it forth," he said. "The head. The truth. You were never meant to wear that human face forever."

Aaron shook violently, every instinct in his body screaming to surrender, to let it happen just so the pain would stop.

But something inside him *refused*.

Not courage.

Not strength.

Something unfinished.

Aaron roared, not fire, not sound, just raw defiance torn out of his chest.

The transformation stalled.

His face snapped back, human, gasping, drenched in sweat.

The pressure held him there, choking, but the change would not come.

Petros frowned.

Just slightly.

"That's…" Petros murmured. "Unexpected."

He tightened his grip, testing.

Nothing.

Aaron dangled there, shaking, wings spasming and folding in, throat crushed, but still human.

Petros studied him now with a different interest.

"You're incomplete," Petros said slowly. "Or protected."

He glanced around the tunnel, senses reaching outward, searching for a variable he hadn't accounted for.

Behind Aaron, the air *shifted*.

Not loudly.

Not visibly.

Just enough.

Petros felt it a fraction of a second too late.

A ripple rolled through the tunnel walls, subtle as a shiver through glass. Sound muted, as if the cave had swallowed it. The darkness deepened even though nothing physically dimmed.

At the moment, all Petros could see, was darkness. "What?"

The lean man froze.

The big one's grin slipped.

"What" the big one began, but then he froze as well.

Aaron felt it too, a sudden relief in his skull as he fell to the ground, pressure lifting like a weight removed.

A voice spoke.

Not loud.

Not dramatic.

Just close enough to make the hair on Aaron's arms rise.

"Move."

A figure stepped from the shadow behind Aaron as if she had always been there.

Not glowing.

Not floating.

Just... present.

A young woman in dark clothing, hood low, eyes steady and unreadable.

Tyler stared at her like she was either an angel or another nightmare.

"Who" Tyler started as he ran over and helped Aaron stand.

The woman cut him off without looking at him. "Not now."

Aaron turned toward her, stunned. "Are you...?"

"You don't have time," she started, voice controlled. "And neither do I."

The tunnel bent.

Not visually.

More like the space itself decided it didn't want the henchmen here.

The woman reached out and grabbed Aaron's wrist.

Her fingers were cold.

"Wings," she said.

Aaron blinked. "What?"

"Use them," she snapped, irritation breaking through her calm. "You control them. That's why you're still alive."

Tyler grabbed Aaron's other arm like he was afraid to let go.

FALAP.

The woman exhaled once.

The world folded.

Aaron felt his stomach drop as if the floor had vanished.

For a fraction of a second, there was no cave, no desert, no sound.

Just darkness.

Then—

They slammed into air.

Not falling, standing.

Aaron staggered, catching himself on a low wall.

Streetlights flickered overhead.

A quiet residential road.

The smell of asphalt and sprinklers.

Tyler fell to his knees immediately and dry-heaved. "I'm gonna throw up. I'm actually gonna throw up."

Aaron's wings twitched and then folded tight into his back as if embarrassed they existed.

He spun toward the woman.

"Sorrie Cerhess?" he asked, voice raw.

6

SHE DIDN'T ANSWER immediately.

Her eyes were on the night, listening, feeling, measuring.

Finally, she looked back at him.

"Yes," she said. "And if you say my name that loud again, I'll disappear."

"So what do we call you?" asked Tyler.

Sorrie just shook her head. "Just call me...Sorceress."

"But isn't that like still your name but condensed?" asked Aaron.

"Call us Aragon," blurted Tyler as they both just looked at him. "Him...call him Aragon!"

"That's not my name!"

Sorrie turned and smiled. "It actually fits!"

She started walking and they followed.

Tyler wiped his mouth. "You...Sorceress...how'd you do that? You just...yoinked us out of a cave."

Sorrie's eyes flicked to Tyler.

"You're loud," she said. "And mouthy!"

"You have no idea," added Aaron.

Tyler blinked. "I'm traumatized."

Sorrie looked back to Aaron.

Aaron's chest heaved. "They were going to...he was making my face..."

"I know," interrupted Sorrie, and her tone sharpened. "And you're lucky it didn't take."

"Lucky?" Aaron snapped. His fear turned into anger fast. "Lucky? My head almost turned into...into a..."

"A full dragon head?" Sorrie finished, and her gaze hardened. "Yes. He tried. Don't use any of your dragon abilities, and he won't be able to just track you."

"I...I can only control my wings, I can't control when I change anything else," started Aaron, "the changes, they just happen randomly, like if I need to do something."

"Your dragon form's instinctual," nodded Sorrie, "that can be problematic!"

"Can you help me control my transformations?" asked Aaron.

Sorrie shook her head in the negative. "I'm not really here for that. Besides, your changes are influenced by instinct and will, I don't mess with those things."

Aaron then started frowning.

"What I can do," started Sorrie, "is shield you when you do change so that Petros can't detect you, but I don't know the spell, I'll need some time. Just try not to change in the meantime, if you do, death will follow."

Aaron clenched his fists. "Who the hell are they anyway?"

Sorrie's expression didn't soften.

"Petros is a demi-god," she said. "He's trying to obtain your dragon flame after your death in order to ascend beyond."

Tyler pushed himself up, shaking. "So what now? Because I vote we call the police."

Sorrie stared at him.

Then she gave the smallest, driest laugh.

"The police can't arrest what doesn't play by mortal rules," she said. "But you can beat him."

Aaron's breath caught. "Me?"

They stopped walking.

"You," she said again, and stepped closer. "Not today. Not tomorrow. But soon, if you stop treating this like something happening *to* you and start realizing what you truly are."

Aaron swallowed, the weight of her words hitting harder than the henchmen's fists.

Tyler looked between them. "Okay, I'm just gonna say what we're all thinking...are you gonna train him?"

Sorrie's eyes stayed on Aaron.

"I'm not here to save you," she said. "I'm here to keep you from dying before you learn how to fight back."

Aaron's jaw tightened. "Learn?"

Sorrie held his gaze. "Do not expose your wings, do not try to look too far out of your normal visual range, don't expose a nail...don't so much as let a dragon scale pop out until next we meet...Aragon!"

Aaron felt his wings twitch from within his back again, reacting to the idea like it was a promise.

She then looked behind him at his torn shirt, shredded from his arm growth and wing exposure in the cave. She waved a hand, "Vestimentum intaurare!"

Aaron's clothes started mending themselves.

"Whoa," started Tyler.

"Wait," started Aaron, "Can I do that?"

"Actually yes," started Sorrie, "but don't try to use magic yet, dragon magic has a scent that Petros can detect."

"You gonna teach him how to use magic to kick Ponytail's but?" asked Tyler.

"Dragon magic is different than sorcery," started Sorrie. "It only affects the dragon directly, meaning you can only use it on yourself."

"Well that sucks!" started Aaron.

"Not if you learn how to use it right," replied Sorrie.

In the distance, somewhere far behind them, a dog barked once.

Sorrie turned her head slightly, listening to something none of them could hear.

Then she looked back at Aaron.

"Next time," she said quietly, "you don't run to the desert."

Aaron frowned. "Why not?"

Sorrie's voice dropped, deadly calm.

"Because the desert remembers dragons. Go home, I'll be in touch...and no more dragon reveals."

The dog barked again.

Tyler and Aaron turned in response.

"So when will we see you again?" asked Aaron as they both turned back to face Sorrie.

She was gone.

"Sorceress?" whispered Tyler.

"C'mon," started Aaron, "I think we have a long walk home!"

7

PETROS HATED UNCERTAINTY.

But it clung to him now like a thin film of oil, invisible but impossible to ignore.

The home he stood in, a rancher, he assumed ownership from through the Arizona State Trilateral Commission so as not to have to deal with hotels, was meant to inspire control.

A private basement underneath the property, which was three times the size of the rancher, afforded the sanctuary and quiet planning space he needed.

Marble floors reflected the soft amber glow of recessed lighting. Sculptures that were originals, and not replicas, stood spaced with intentional restraint. A grand desk of black glass and brushed steel dominated the far end of the room. The ceiling, an astonishing thirty feet.

At the far end of the room there was a twenty-foot-wide slanted upward ramp which led out to the outside through the ground which had a recessed access way, probably developed for an intended purpose in the past but never repurposed or sold.

Petros would make plans for it if he had planned to stay long but he didn't. Once he was done with Skylar's last descendant and acquired his flame, he would be a God and no longer need to stay on this planet. He would leave this place and any cash he had amassed to his loyal henchmen.

But for now, this was his sanctuary. His temporary war room. A place where plans would be devised so problems would end.

Yet Petros stood motionless near a large wall-enclosed fish tank, hands clasped behind his back, staring at the fish as if they had personally offended him.

Behind him, his two cronies waited.

Both were extremely loyal. Both, in over thirty-five hundred years of them working for him, he never doubted that they were true to him. Both were enhanced by Petros which has elongated their lifespans well beyond what they were supposed to live. But now, both had failed him.

"You were there," Petros said calmly, without turning around. His voice was measured, cultured, dangerous in its restraint. "Both of you. Close enough to smell the water in the cave. Close enough to see him move, to touch him and his human friend."

Byron, the taller of the two, broad-shouldered, his posture unnaturally rigid, shifted uncomfortably. Faint veins of magic pulsed beneath his skin, a side effect of the power augmentation which had made him more weapon than man.

"Yes," Byron confirmed. "We saw him."

Petros smiled thinly. "And?"

Cage, the second henchman frowned, his brow furrowing as if the effort itself caused pain.

"We saw something else too," Cage offered slowly. "But every time I tried to look at the boy..." He stopped, frustrated, pressing his fingers to his temple. "It was like...looking... at... smoke."

Petros finally turned.

His dark eyes flicked between them, sharp and analytical. He approached, studying their faces the way a scientist might study flawed data.

"You are both telling me," Petros said, "that you were present at the moment my target vanished... after yall chased him out of the mall and into the desert, and grabbed him in a cave, and yet you cannot tell me what he looks like?"

"To be fair boss," started Byron, "You had your hand around his neck and you don't remember either!"

Petros quickly side kicked Byron to the other side of the room, back first into a wall.

Byron fell.

"DID I ASK FOR YOUR COMMENT?"

There was silence as Byron picked himself up off the floor.

"That is...very inconvenient," Petros continued softly as he composed himself. "You see, about thirty-five hundred years ago, I selected you two specifically to stay with me because of your ruthlessness and cunning when hunting for me. Your uncanny ability to assist me in getting my job done has kept me content thus far." His head shaking yes and then his smile faded. "So if *you* are unable to assist me any longer..."

He moved past them toward his desk, fingers gliding across the surface. "...why would I need you any longer?"

He exhaled through his nose.

The taller henchman hesitated. "Sir... it feels intentional. Like something is blocking us. Not erasing memory, redirecting it."

Petros paused.

That was the moment.

The realization slid into place, cold and precise.

"This was definitely not stealth," Petros said quietly. "And it isn't chance."

He straightened, eyes gleaming with renewed focus.

"This is protection," offered Cage.

"This kid is not hiding himself," Petros continued. "Someone is hiding *him*."

The second henchman looked up. "His accomplice?"

"He didn't look to be of any significance to me," Petros replied, "but maybe he is something to consider for now."

"A constant. Something has power, or someone else, can latch onto his maybe?"

Petros turned sharply to Byron. "But you did remember something, didn't you?"

Both men stilled.

"He had an accomplice," Petros said. "The one who was *there with him*."

The second henchman swallowed. "Yes. Him... the one with the loudmouth, I can see him. Clearer than the one we want."

Petros's smile returned, "this one is human, he can be tracked by their laws and systems."

He gestured toward the far end of the room, where a circular dais lay dormant, etched with symbols too old to be decorative and too precise to be art.

"Sit," Petros ordered.

The man obeyed, uneasy.

"This will not hurt," Petros said, already rolling back his sleeves. "Much."

He began tracing sigils in the air, each one igniting briefly before fading into the next. The temperature in the room shifted. The lights dimmed, not flickered, but *yielded*.

"Do not try to remember the dragon boy," Petros instructed. "You won't be able to. Someone has ensured that." His voice lowered. "Instead, remember the *other one*. The friend. The ordinary one."

The man's eyes glazed as the magic took hold.

"Describe him," Petros said.

As the henchman spoke, the air above the dais shimmered. Lines formed. Shadows gained structure. A face began to emerge, imperfect at first, wavering, then sharpening as Petros anchored the spell.

A human face. Unremarkable. And therefore dangerous.

Petros studied it with satisfaction.

"Now," he murmured, activating his computer as the magical construct stabilized, "let's see where you lead me."

The computer clicked on and streams of data surged to life, magic feeding technology, technology refining information disseminated from magic, facial recognition, social networks, public records, digital footprints awakening all at once.

Petros sat at the desk and clasped his hands behind his back, watching the data build up on the screen.

Thanks to Tyler being a tech wizard, his digital trail was difficult to find, but not impossible as fragments started to surface.

"Young dragon boy," he said softly, almost fondly. "If I cannot see you...I will simply follow the young man standing next to you."

"And when I find him..."

He smiled.

"I will find you."

8

THE SUN HAD not fully risen and yet the warmth of the barren desert could already be felt.

Tyler sat a box of donuts and a cup holder with three coffees on a large boulder next to where he was standing.

Aaron shook his head in the negative. "Who brings coffee to a desert?"

"Dude, she had us meet at a mall," argued Tyler. "How was I supposed to know she'd bring us here?"

Sorrie smiled. "Alright Aragon!"

"Okay Sorceress," replied Aragon.

"Hey everyone, I'm Tyler!" waved Tyler.

Aaron laughed.

"Did he really need to be here?" asked Sorrie.

"If not for him, I wouldn't have found you so..."

"I'm his Techkick!"

"His what?" asked Sorrie.

"Something he came up with," said Aaron.

"Yeah," started Tyler, "since he is technically not inclined, I'm his computer man...instead of a sidekick, a techkick!"

Sorrie just shook her head in the negative. "Well we technik -ly don't need you."

"It's Techkick, not technik," corrected Tyler.

"Whatever," started Sorrie. "First, Aragon, I'm going to enchant you..." She touched his forehead and both sides of his face. "This will blur out any dragon noise so Petros nor his henchmen can sense you when any of your dragon parts become revealed."

Aaron nodded his understanding.

"This will only last for a few hours so our session will be brief."

"Since when is a few hours brief?" asked Tyler.

"Pay no attention to the idiot near the boulder," said Aragon trying to sound like the wizard from the movie, 'Wizard of Oz.'

Sorrie chuckled and Aragon immediately noticed her beauty up close.

"Now I'm going to give you a spell..."

"Similar to the one you gave me for my clothes?"

"Yes, but this one is for your body," she said. "Use it sparingly, I don't know the effects of overusing it."

"Sounds uncanny."

"Sanatio Corpus Meus!"

"Sanatio Corpus Meus!" repeated Aragon.

"Good," replied Sorrie, "when you get hurt in either human or dragon form, this is how you will heal yourself."

Tyler shook his head in the affirmative while watching and eating a donut and drinking a cup of coffee.

"Now let's start with something we know you can control," started Sorrie. "WINGS OUT!"

Without hesitation, Aragons' wings ripped through the rear of shirt and sprouted quickly from his back.

"When I say go, I want you to go straight up and then fly to that cliff all the way over there, swoop around and then arch your wings back, fly quickly past me and then land at the base of that wall, retract your wings and jump up onto that cliff."

"This will be cake," started Aragon, we already know I can fly."

"GO!"

Without hesitation Aragon took off, straight up. and then-

FALAP-

he headed in the direction of the cliff.

FALAP

"WHOO HOO!" he yelled as the warm breeze caressed him as he flew effortlessly through the sky.

FALAP

He soon reached the cliff and circled above it in two long circles, keeping his wingspan extended and simply gliding as if he were a giant kite.

Aragon then headed back in the other direction, starting with a large FALAP and then arching his wings back as instructed and speeding towards the other cliff.

Sorrie started flailing her arms as she immediately grew concerned. "ARAGON SLOW DOWN!"

"DUDE...YOU'RE GONNA CRASH!" yelled Tyler.

"OPEN YOUR WINGS!" yelled Sorrie.

Aragon spread his wings a little too late and crashed into the canyon wall.

"DUDE...SAY THE SPELL!" yelled Tyler.

***

"Alright," started Sorrie, "so we'll revisit the flying thing later, we really wanted to focus on your transformations anyway! Do you remember how you were feeling when you were running from those two henchmen?"

"Scared shitless," yelled Tyler.

"Defensive," Aragon corrected.

"I can work with either one," started Sorrie. "Okay, show me dragon hands!"

"What?" asked Aaron.

"Dragons don't have hands," started Tyler, "what kind of sorceress are you?"

Sorrie sighed. "For the love of...we don't have time!"

Sorrie waved her hand forward and pebbles and rocks from the ground started advancing quickly towards Aragon.

Without warning the rocks started growing into large boulders.

"Oh my God no!" yelled Aragon as his arms tore through the sleeves of hi long sleeved shirt and quickly morphed into the large dragon claws and he effortlessly swatted the first two boulders away.

He then slammed his nails into the next two boulders and held them up. "YO TYLER CHECK IT OUT!"

Tyler threw a thumbs up and then his eyes widened. "Yo dude!"

Aragon stopped smiling and looked ahead just in time to see a large boulder coming directly at him and he turned around and suddenly a large tail busted out of the rear of his pants and slammed down on the boulder causing each half to veer away from him.

Aragon turned around as he was finally able to drop the boulders. "Look Tyler, a tail!"

Tyler smiled as Sorrie looked over at him and mouthed, *dragon...hands*!

"Alright Aragon," started Sorrie while clapping her hands, " I need you to focus now!"

Aragon faced her smilingly. "Ready!"

"Try flexing your talons only," started Sorrie. "Do not move your wrist at all!"

Aragon smiled. "Seems simple enough!"

He tried flexing the talons but kept flexing his wrist.

"NO!" she yelled. "NOT THE WRISTS, ONLY YOUR TALONS!"

Aragon tried multiple times but was unable to complete the task.

"OKAY, OKAY," she started as she moved closer to him. "Let's try something that should be a little easier."

"Try shifting your tail without moving your spine!"

Aragon swayed his hips from left to right, doing the opposite of what Sorrie instructed."

"No, no Aragon," she started, keep your hips still and try just to move your tail."

Aragon started moving and appeared to be doing a hoola-hoop."

"Dude, where's your rhythm?" asked Tyler.

Sorrie smiled as she got an idea and moved closer to a frustrated Aragon.

"I'm sorry," started Aragon as Sorrie moved towards him. " I appreciate you helpin' me and all but maybe it's no use."

"Hey, hey, hey," started Sorrie, "Don't say that! You literally just learned within the last week that, that you're a dragon who someone wants to kill! I think you are doing good all things considered. Besides, you might just need a little inspiration!"

Sorrie snapped her fingers and soft ballroom music, *'The Blue Danube'*, started playing. "Gimmie you claws!"

Aragon started reaching for her hand with his claws.

"Be gentle," she said as they started dancing.

Tyler developed a strange look on his face.

"Where's this music coming from?" he asked.

Sorrie led Aragon in a dance, and they looked into each other's eyes and smiled.

Aragon looked down with slight embarrassment and then back up at Sorrie. "You know," I really appreciate everything you've been doing for me...especially with saving my life an all!"

Sorrie smiled. "Thank me when you defeat Petros!"

"I appreciate everything anyway!"

Sorrie smiled. "You're welcome! I bet you didn't know you were twirling your tail around back there!"

"What?" asked Aragon in disbelief as he stopped dancing and turned to look at his tail.

The music stopped.

Sorrie laughed. "Tail in!"

Aragon retracted his tail.

"Wings out!"

Aragon released and expanded his wings.

"Wings in!"

Aragon retracted his wings.

"Claws in!"

Aragon changed his claws into his regular hands.

"Claws out!"

He automatically brough forth his dragon claws and hands.

"Claws in!"

Aragon again changed his claws into his regular hands.

"Now," started Sorrie, "I want you to run towards those two boulders, morph with your arms tail, and wings in place, arched straight back, pick up those boulders and fly them to that first cliff you flew to and drop them off and then come back here."

"And that's it?"

"That's it," smiled Sorrie.

Aragon turned and ran towards the boulders and just before he reached them, on command, his wings came out, arched straight back, his tail grew out and lifted as he ran and he jumped up and came down over the boulders just as his hands morphed into the giant claws.

He dug his nails into the boulders and then-

FALAP-

He flew straight up!

Sorrie covered her mouth laughing.

"YES!" exclaimed Tyler as he watched his friend fly higher and higher.

Aragon climbed higher, the boulders vibrating in his grip as his wings beat a steady rhythm.

Then the air changed.

Not suddenly, not violently, but *wrong*.

The warmth beneath him vanished as a pocket of cold air surged upward through the canyon, slamming into his left wing while the right caught a rising thermal. His body twisted mid-beat.

"ARAGON...STEADY!" Sorrie shouted.

He tried.

Instinct took over before control could. His wings flared unevenly, his tail snapped hard to compensate, and the boulders shifted in his claws. Panic tightened his chest, stealing the breath Sorrie had warned him never to lose.

"DUDE...YOU'RE LOSING IT!" Tyler yelled.

Aragon felt the rhythm break.

The wind roared once—then dropped out from under him entirely.

He fell fast.

Too fast.

Sorrie threw her hands upward, murmuring a sharp incantation as a translucent force slowed his descent just enough to keep the impact from killing him.

Aragon still hit hard.

The ground slammed into his side, knocking the air from his lungs. The boulders tore free from his grasp and shattered against the canyon floor. His wings sprawled awkwardly behind him, trembling.

He coughed, pain blooming white-hot through his leg and ribs. Blood spotted the sand as he wheezed, unable to pull in a full breath.

"Aragon!" Tyler started forward.

"Stop," Sorrie ordered sharply, dropping beside Aragon. "Listen to me."

His eyes darted wildly. "I...I can't..."

"Yes, you can," she said, gripping his shoulder. "Slow. Deep breaths. Just like before."

He obeyed, trembling.

"Now close your eyes," she said gently. "Say it."

Aragon squeezed his eyes shut.

"Sanatio Corpus Meus."

Warmth immediately spread outward from his chest, dulling the pain, knitting muscle and bone. His wings shuddered once...then folded inward, dissolving as his body returned fully to human form.

He lay there for a moment, breathing.

He then stood up and wiped the blood from around his mouth. "Thank you, Sorceress," he said.

Tyler hugged him. "Dude, I'm so glad you're okay!"

"Why don't we call it a day," suggested Sorrie!

"I agree," said Aaron.

Tyler raised his hand. "Uh...before we go back to the mall, Aragon here might want to use that other spell! His entire ass is showing over here!"

9

THE FIRST RULE of hunting was patience.

The second was knowing when not to be seen.

Stakeouts were supposed to be boring.

Byron had learned long ago that boredom was a luxury, one he no longer trusted.

He sat behind the wheel of a nondescript sedan parked half a block from a small neighborhood park, sunglasses on despite the overcast sky. In the passenger seat, Cage remained perfectly still, his gaze fixed forward, posture relaxed in a way that only came from centuries of waiting.

"This is him?" Cage asked without looking away.

Byron nodded. "Tyler. Tyler Landon. Last name took a while. He's careful. Digital footprint's messy, by design. But he is not invisible."

Cage exhaled slowly. "Humans," he said. "Always the weakest link."

Across the street, Tyler sat on a bench with a backpack at his feet, phone nowhere in sight. He laughed suddenly, loud and unguarded, then leaned back as if someone beside him had said something particularly stupid.

Byron frowned.

"Talking to himself?" Cage asked.

"Looks like it."

They watched.

Tyler gestured with his hands while speaking, animated, reactive. He paused, nodded, then laughed again, this time quieter. A jogger passed. A woman walked her dog. No one paid him any attention.

Byron felt an itch start behind his eyes.

"People don't talk like that to themselves," Cage said.

"They do when they're lonely."

Cage turned his head slightly. "He doesn't look lonely to me."

***

"Dude, you were flying like crazy fast!" laughed Tyler as Aaron moved out of the way of the jogger.

"Yo keep it down on all that flying talk," cautioned Aaron. "Sorceress said we need to be as cool and discreet as possible."

"I know, I know, I'm sorry man, but seeing you in action just had me so pumped up!"

Aaron smiled a little. "Yeah it was kinda cool though, wasn't it?"

A woman walked past with a small dog which paid them no mind.

"And for reals though," I think this Sorrie chick kinda got a thing for you!"

"Tyler she is like, eight years older than me...she's just a good teacher!"

"Look at you," started Tyler as he laughed, "You even doin' the math in your head already about how far apart you are, that proves you like her."

"It don't matter what I like," protested Aaron, "she's tryin' to save my life and I'm grateful."

Tyler looked at his watch. "C'mon lets go to my house, I'm getting a little hungry and all this sitting around and waiting to die stuff is bad for my nerves."

"Yeah," agreed Aaron, "something about sitting out here in the open is giving me the chills."

They then left from out of the park.

***

Byron and cage followed Tyler home that afternoon.

From across the street, the house was unremarkable. Small. Clean. Curtains open. Tyler moved through rooms with purpose, occasionally stopping, turning his head as if listening.

Waiting.

Responding.

At one point, he stood in the kitchen holding a glass of water, staring at an empty space near the counter.

Then he smiled.

Byron lowered his binoculars. "You see that?"

Cage nodded. "I see what I don't see."

They then witnessed as the front door to Tyler's house opened for a moment, and they soon adjusted themselves in the seat, wondering if they were spotted.

A moment later they saw Tyler's head pop out.

"School tomorrow, yup!"

Byron and Cage just looked at each other.
"What?" asked Cage.

***

"So you think she will spaz out?" asked Tyler as he got a glass of water.

"Oh I know she will," started Aaron, "this whole, I'm a dragon and a four thousand plus year old man is trying to take off my head so he can be a God thing would give her a heart attack."

Tyler nodded in understanding as he drunk the water.

"My only saving grace," continued Aaron, "Is that she's a surgeon with a crazy busy schedule."

"If one of my parents was a surgeon," started Tyler, " I'd be wearing way better gear than that, he said pointing at Aaron.

"Ha, ha, ha," started Aaron. "speaking of which, I better get home, my mom will be in soon and I told her I would start dinner when I got home."

They walked out the kitchen and Aaron opened the door and looked out. He then headed home. "See you at school tomorrow!"

"School tomorrow, yup!" Tyler yelled back.

***

Monday rolled around and at the end of the day, Aaron and Tyler came out of the building along with the rest of the students.

"Are you really getting your schoolwork done?" asked Aaron because you seem to talk a lot about Aragon."

"C'mon Aaron," started an animated Tyler. "It'd be just like that scene in Shazam where

Shazam and Superman show up in the cafeteria for Freddy Freeman!"

Aaron looked over near the main quad and saw maintenance workers. "Must be another busted pipe," he said,

He then laughed at Tyler. "That would be pretty cool!"

"Right, Right?"

"They come burstin' in the gym behind me just to get their shorts muddied."

Aaron laughed and they gave each other a high five as the other kids walked around them.

***

Monday seemed like it would be unproductive, but they went to the school to watch him anyway.

Busy. Loud. Safe.

The kind of place no one expected to be watched.

They positioned themselves near the main quad, blending in easily, they were maintenance workers today, reflective vests and clipboards.

Tyler exited the school building with a group of other students, laughing, walking backwards as he talked.

Byron's attention sharpened.

Tyler stopped.

Turned slightly to his right.

Raised his hand.

And high-fived empty air.

Why did he high five empty air? That was a human concept usually done between friends.

Clean. Familiar. Casual.

No one paid attention to it like he'd done it in front of them a hundred times before, slapping empty air.

Cage went very still.

"There," he said.

Tyler continued walking, still talking, still reacting. Students walked around an empty space, almost as if something were there. None of them noticing Tyler talking to himself.

Byron swallowed. "He's not alone."

"No," Cage replied. "He's not."

They stood there longer than necessary, watching Tyler fade into the crowd, still half-turned, still speaking, still smiling at someone who could not be seen, by them.

Byron finally exhaled. "So that's how they hide him."

Cage's lips curled faintly. "Only from us

Byron looked at him.

"They keep us from seeing him."

Byron thought of the cave. The smoke in his mind. How things moved real slow. The blank space where a face should have been.

"Petros was right," he said quietly. "We don't need to see the dragon."

Cage nodded once.

"We just follow the friend."

They turned away from the quad, already planning the next phase, not pursuit, not confrontation.

Just patience. Continuing to not be seen.

And giving it time.

10

THE FIRST SIGN they were being followed wasn't dramatic.

It was just the kind of scenario she would have expected from someone who had money, resources, henchmen, and time.

Her fuzz spell worked perfect on Aaron and had he'd been a loner; he would've never been made. But Aaron wasn't alone, he had Tyler with him.

She couldn't even be mad at him though, because as he put it, he'd never would've found her had it not been for Tyler's help.

Little did Aaron know, they almost got him, because of his friends' presence.

She sat high above the Barrio Queen and watched as Tyler and Aaron were mindful of the traffic as they crossed the parking lot oblivious to the black sedan following them.

Tyler was being his usual loud and extra self which made him an even more interesting candidate to observe because to Petros and his cohorts, Tyler would appear to be talking to himself.

Sorrie, in her dark hoodie and jeans nodded in the negative as she made her way to their planned meeting spot.

Below in the parking lot, the Sedan pulled into one of the available spots.

Byron and Cage exited the vehicle and made their way into the mall.

***

Aaron and Tyler made their way through the mall and headed into the Dave & Busters as instructed by Sorrie.

As they made their way through the gaming section, they were both tapped on the shoulder by Sorrie, and they jumped as they turned around, and were relieved it was her.

Sorrie looked at Tyler. "You're loud!"

"Why does everyone keep saying that? "He asked.

"Told you so," said Aaron.

Sorrie took her hand and tapped them each on the shoulder and then her hand switched shoulders.

***

Aaron immediately looked around smiling at the comfort while Tyler went to covering his eyes due to the blinding light and the desert heat.

She removed her hood and unzipped her jacket.

"They see you Aaron," she said.

Aaron turned and faced her quickly.

"Wait...what?"

"More accurately," she started as she nodded her head in Tyler's direction. "They see him."

"Me?" asked Tyler.

"Yes you...Tech... kick," started Sorrie.

"I don't like how you said that," said Tyler.

88

"They must have somehow remembered what you looked like the other day and used your image to find you."

Sorrie then threw her arms up and flailed them around. "But all this," she said, not intending to be funny but causing Aaron to chuckle, "This is what made them keep watching you! You walk around in their eyes alone, but you always look as if you're having a conversation."

Tyler looked away disappointed.

"So, he stops coming with us," started Aaron.

"Wait," protested Tyler, "no!"

"We can't do that now," started Sorrie.

"Yeah, what she said," agreed Tyler."

Aaron held his hand out towards him.

"We stop him from coming, he's no longer involved, he's safe. End of story!"

"No," started Sorrie, "he's past the safe zone. They absolutely have his face, and they absolutely know that he is connected to you, if you cut him loose now, they will use him to bait you, and likely will kill you both."

"Oh shit!" exclaimed Tyler.

"So whatta we do?" asked Aaron.

"You stay close to him, we keep training! Get you ready to defend yourself!"

"You get quiet!" she said pointing at Tyler. "At this point if you stop talking to him while out in public, they'll believe you two aren't together at the moment, and they will keep watching your movements and patterns. They need to continue to believe you are as ignorant about them watching you as you act."

"Now what is that supposed to mean?" asked Tyler sounding offended.

"And you Aragon," started Sorrie, "we up your training game, starting tomorrow."

"Why not today?" asked Aaron.

"Tyler's new friends are looking for him at the Dave & Busters right now."

"Shit," whispered Tyler.

"They need to see you leaving so that all they continue to do is observe. After you get home, text me your address and tomorrow I will come and get you two while they sit outside your home."

Aaron smiled. "I like that plan."

***

At the Dave & Busters, the bathroom door opened and Aaron walked out followed by Tyler and they moved between the two henchmen when Aaron accidently bumped into one of them, Byron, who quickly turned around.

"Scuse me sir," Tyler said quickly as Cage turned around and the pair watched him as he left out of the activity center.

They both quickly went to the door and continued to watch Tyler from the door.

They then looked at each other and then back at Tyler.

Through clenched lips and without bringing any additional attention to himself Tyler asked, "are they following us?"

While walking backwards and looking at the door Aaron answered, "no, not yet." He then turned around. "But just keep walking and act natural, because at some point, they will!"

11

AS SORRIE EXPECTED, Tyler's unsolicited babysitters were parked outside of his home, prior to the start of the school day.

Tyler faked being sick and since he had perfect grades, his parents weren't too concerned with him taking one sick day. He assured them he would be fine, nothing a one-day break from school couldn't resolve.

Aaron, on the other hand, left his house for school as usual and arrived at his friends' home a little while after Tyler's parents left. He used the back door to enter so the henchmen wouldn't figure out that invisible Aaron went into the house.

Tyler positioned some pillows and clothing on his bed in a specific way as to make anyone who was looking in his window think someone was still sleeping in the bed.

"Nice," started Aaron while peering into the room.

Tyler flicked his shirt collar and sucked his teeth. "Your boy got skills!"

"What are you doing?" asked Aaron as he moved past him towards the basement steps.

"Looking for a new image," started Tyler as he followed Aaron down the basement steps."

Aaron stared at him as they met Sorrie in the basement.

"No," he said.

Sorrie touched their shoulders.

***

Tyler sat next to the large boulder and shaded himself from the sun.

"We're gonna test your hand-to-hand combat skills," started Sorrie.

Aragon smiled and did a little dancing foot work while dodging nothing. "You don't want none of this!"

Sorrie laughed. "Not me," she started as she pointed behind him. "Them!"

Aragon turned around and saw five beings behind him who looked as if they literally just came up from the dirt themselves and he jumped, "Jesus!"

"Shit, where the hell did they come from?" asked Tyler. "Dirt soldiers...doldiers...doldiers."

Aragon shook his head in the negative. *Tyler's need to name everything,* he thought.

Sorrie continued. "Don't worry Aragon, they have no souls, so you can't kill them. Their sole purpose is to bring you down."

"What, I don't get a weapon?"

"Not yet," started Sorrie. "What good is having a weapon if you can't even fight hand to hand?"

Aaron cracked his neck from left to right. "Okay...lets do this!"

The first doldier dove into him and knocked him down.

92

Aaron tussled with him and then the remaining four all dove on him.

Sorrie shook her head in the negative as all the doldiers collapsed into dust over him.

Aragon looked up at Sorrie as he brushed the dust off the front of his hair.

"Let's try this again, shall we?" asked Sorrie.

***

The next day, Aaron sat in his class and was finishing up filling out a scantron answer sheet when he happened to look out the class window and across the parking lot at the side street.

He was certain he was looking at the sedan which had been following Tyler as of late, their vehicle pointed in the direction of the other end of the school.

He started to worry. It was one thing when it was his own life that was in danger, but Tyler really was just a kid, and he didn't deserve any of this.

Aaron developed an angry look on his face as he just stared at the car.

***

Back at the desert the next evening, Aaron was moving really good against the doldiers, ducking when he needed to, punching and kicking with a side spin without effort. After knocking down the last one of the doldiers, he slammed his fist downward, pulverizing his fist into the ground.

He then looked at Sorrie and smiled.

"That's' real good Aragon!" she then pointed behind him. "Now how about taking care of them."

Ten more Doldiers were running towards Aragon.

Aragon looked down at his fist and sighed. He then got up just in time to catch a doldier arm coming down over him and he flipped the creature as he quickly stood up and caught the punch of another one.

He countered, he spun, he kicked, and dropped he was holding his own pretty well.

Sorrie smiled impressed. She waved more doldiers to him as Tyler just grinned wildly.

"NO!" yelled Aragon, "Too much, too soon!"

***

The next day at school, Aaron and Tyler sat side by side in the quiet corner of the school library, a row of computers glowing softly in front of them. The faint hum of the machines blended with the occasional turning of a page somewhere deeper in the room.

Tyler leaned forward in his chair, fingers moving quickly across the keyboard as he explained what he was doing.

“See, computers don’t actually *think*,” Tyler said matter-of-factly. “They just follow instructions. The trick is learning how to give them the right ones.”

Aaron watched the screen carefully, nodding as he listened. Tyler slid his chair slightly to the side so Aaron could move in front of the keyboard.

“Alright, your turn,” Tyler said. “Just type what I told you.”

Aaron hesitated for only a moment before placing his fingers on the keys. Slowly, carefully, he began typing the lines of code Tyler had shown him, stopping occasionally to glance at the notebook Tyler had scribbled instructions into.

"Good," Tyler encouraged quietly. "Now hit enter."

Aaron pressed the key.

For a brief second nothing happened.

Then the small program executed exactly as Tyler had promised it would.

Aaron leaned back slightly, surprised at how easily the computer obeyed the commands he had just written.

Tyler grinned.

"See? Told you. You just programmed your first piece of code."

Aaron looked at the screen again, then at Tyler.

A slow smile spread across his face.

Without a word, the two of them raised their hands and slapped a quick high five between them, the sound echoing softly through the quiet library.

Aaron looked back at the screen, a little more confident now.

"Okay," he said, cracking his knuckles lightly. "What's next?"

Tyler's grin widened.

"Oh man," he said. "Now the fun part starts."

***

Back at the desert, Aragon had become quite proficient at defeating the doldiers, so Sorrie upped the game a bit, making them twice the mass and twice as strong, Aragon held his own,

but he was obviously starting to struggle as he
was getting slowed down in his fights.

"Okay Aragon," started Sorrie, "it's time to
start letting your dragon side help you out a little!
Mentally call out the body part you want to help
you!"

Aragon smiled as a doldier dove in his
direction and he reached his left hand forward as
it morphed in a large red reptilian dragon claw
and caught the doldier by the neck.

He then quickly slammed the doldier down
through the ground.

One flew up and over from the back.

His large tail shot through the rear of his
pants and intercepted the doldier through the
chest, destroying it.

Two from either side.

Two lizard arms caught each of them and he
spun around and threw them each a hundred
yards in each direction.

"No way!" exclaimed Tyler excitedly.

Sorrie laughed.

A bunch of them jumped on him and covered
him up but then Aragon jumped straight up with
the doldiers still holding onto him and his wings
spanned outward.

FALAP! and he took off with the doldiers
falling off of him and turning back into the desert
dust as they hit the ground.

This time he flew around the canyon with
increased confidence, adjusting to every change
in the wind currents, dipping and angling with
near perfection.

He soon neared Sorrie and Tylers' position as the tale, arms and legs all submerged.

He landed majestically and his wings recessed immediately into his back.

"Vestimentum intaurare!" said Aragon, causing his clothes to repair as he walked towards them.

Tyler started clapping.

Sorrie produced the largest and most beautiful smile.

"Well Sorceress," started Aragon, "how'd I do?"

"You have earned Kusanagi," started Sorrie.

"Say what?" asked Aragon.

"You have mastered, the beast within you," started Sorrie, "Kusanagi is an ancient sword born out of the body of Yamat No Orochi, an eight headed dragon serpent. The sword is meant to protect dragons but cannot be used by dragons. When Petros started his conquest to slay the last dragon and to steal his flame, one of the sorcerers of the past changed the dragon code to blend with human code in order for the order of dragons to have a way to eventually save their blood line. "

"Find the sorceress," started Tyler.

"Yes," started Sorrie, "Aragon, the map to Kusanagi was embedded in your DNA, not merely so you could be trained to fight..."

"...but so I could learn how to tame myself in order to earn the weapon I needed to defeat my enemy."

"Yes," agreed Sorrie.

"So when do I get it," asked Aragon.

Sorrie frowned, realizing he didn't fully understand the concept. "Aragon, Kusanagi isn't a thing you possess, she is a weapon who will come to you when you most need her to protect yourself as long as you have full control of your dragon side."

"Ohhhhhh,"said Aragon and Tyler simultaneously.

12

PETROS DID NOT pace.

Pacing was for lesser beings, those ruled by time instead of mastering it.

Still, something inside him felt...tight.

He stood at the edge of the chamber, hands clasped behind his back, staring into the large fish tank.

"Where are we with the boy...Tyler, is it?" he asked calmly.

Byron stood nearby, arms folded.

Cage leaned against a stone pillar, expression unreadable.

"We initially expected he was talking with the mark," Cage offered. "Responding to nothing, high fivin' the air..."

Petros's eyes narrowed. "Then?"

"Then," started Byron, "he looked like he came down with a sudden case of depression, always moping', goin' to Dave & Buster's by himself, just looking completely miserable. He actually ended up staying home sick the next day...almost feel bad for him."

Petros glared between the two of them. "He went from over exuberant and loud to instantly depressed?"

Cage nodded.

"You were made, idiots!" started Petros as he walked over to Byron and stared hard. "What teen do you know goes to a 'Dave & Busters' just to hang by themself?"

"Well, we just figured he had to go to the bathroom cause that's where he came from when we saw him."

"Yeah," agreed Cage.

"At a shopping mall with hundreds of bathrooms, you think he would pass a perfectly good bathroom outside, go into a crowded...teen hang out...just to use the bathroom?"

Cage shrugged his shoulders. "Well, when you ask it like that..."

"GET THIS TYLER KID AND BRING HIM TO ME!" yelled an angry Petros

"Kidnapping a human child will draw attention," protested Cage. "We might be made before we can get him back here."

Petros turned slowly.

"Killing the last dragon will also bring attention to us," he said softly.

Silence followed.

"Over three weeks have passed and I do not know the dragon's human name yet," said Petros "I do not know his bloodline, his parents remain hidden to me. His protector remains unseen. But this Tyler..." started Petros. "This one is close to the dragon. Close enough to matter."

Cage frowned. "If we take him..."

"Then don't take him," interrupted Petros. "Kill him."

Byron's jaw tightened. "You want the kid dead?"

"That's what killing him means," Petros replied. "If nothing else gets the dragon to look for me, this will do it, and you have to take him when you think he is with the other one! If he is at the school, take him. At the park, take him. IF HE IS AT THE MALL, especially at a Dave & Busters...TAKE HIM!"

A faint smile touched Petros's lips.

"I want him angry; he will shift faster and be unable to control his rage."

"And when the dragon comes?" Cage asked.

Petros's eyes gleamed.

"Then," he started, "he will be ready for me to take his head."

13

THE FIRST THING Aaron felt after the desert heat he lived in during his training exercise was the cool air conditioning from overhead as they walked out the bathroom of the AMC theater.

"Awe c'mon," started Tyler, "just one movie"

Aaron laughed. "We didn't pay; we're not staying!"

"I think the hero thing is startin' to go to your head...I mean, we're already inside."

"I said no"!

They walked out the doors and into the parking lot.

"You are such a buzz kill," cried Tyler.

Aaron thought about this for a minute. "Next time we end up here, one movie,"

"Yes!" Tyler whooped as he started laughing.

One second Tyler was laughing, mid-sentence, the next he was being yanked backward by the collar, quickly pulled toward the black sedan like a package someone had decided to claim.

"HEY!" Aaron shouted as he started running after the car.

Something within him snapped.

The air seemed to have shifted.

The black sedan sped further.

Aaron kept running after the car but couldn't keep up at first. He growled as he stopped and took off in another direction.

***

Inside the car, Byron struggled to hold Tyler steady as Cage kept driving.

"GET OFF ME!" demanded Tyler but only silence answered. "My boy is gonna so come after you!"

"Yeah, that's what we're hoping for kid!" grinned Byron.

***

The sedan turned sharply and was speeding past multiple cars, recklessly when all of a sudden it turned down a long stretch of road which bordered the desert.

"I don't get it," started Cage, "I'd thought we would at least seen him by now?"

THUMP

The car shuddered.

They all three looked at the top of the car.

The rear of the hood started moaning while rolling back towards the front of the car as large red scaly hands could be seen rolling them back until the face of a hybrid red dragon / man could be seen looking down into the car.

Byron yelled. "HE'S ON THE ROOF!"

Tyler closed his eyes. "Oh please let that be Aragon, please let that be Aragon...PLEASE...let this be Aragon!"

The dragon snarled as Cage quickly swerved left and then right, causing the dragon hybrid man to fall off.

Byron recovered fast. Too fast as he then pulled out a switchblade. "Nothin' personal kid!"

"Wait..." cried Tyler as Byron quickly stabbed him three times causing him to scream right before Byron shoved him out of the moving car."

"Now," started Byron while breathing hard, "the trap is set!"

***

Aragon, on the ground in hybrid humanoid /dragon form, picked his head up just as he heard Tyler scream and he roared, taking off on all fours in the direction of the car.

He smelled blood when he saw Tyler's body on the edge of the roadway, barely conscious.

Aragon stopped and sniffed him and Tyler groaned.

"I'll be okay," he said weakly. "Go get them!"

Aragon smiled a little as he turned.

He then hesitated as Tyler nodded his head in the affirmative.

Aragon again then took off on all fours and as he was running, his wings tore out of his back in a straight back racing ark formation.

Then-

FALAP!

He took off in the sky and flew straight for the sedan.

Car horns of the few other cars on the stretch of road honked.

"HERE HE COMES!" yelled Byron as he noticed the anger on Aragon's face as he drew closer.

Byron smiled. "Can't hide from us in this form!"

Aragon flew fast past the car, causing Byron to look up as right before he heard Cage screaming.

The car slammed into something as Byron fell into the empty front seat.

Confused he looked around and observed the bloody windshield

Byron barely had time to register the change in pressure before Aragon grabbed him.

Byron looked on shocked as the humanoid dragon was now an astounding ten feet tall with front claws large enough to wrap around his body.

Horns below honked as some traffic started moving through the area, drivers obviously shocked by the presence they were beholding.

Aragon threw Byron down to the desert floor with one hand and tossed the car far over to the left with the other.

He then roared as he flapped and lowered himself to the ground.

Byron and Cage lay twisted where Aragon had thrown them, breath knocked from their lungs, dust rising slowly around their bodies.

Then the twitching began.

At first it was subtle, a shudder running beneath the skin, as if something inside them was testing the walls of its prison. Their fingers curled inward unnaturally, their joints cracking in sharp, staccato bursts. Their spines arched. Their teeth clenched.

Byron's back convulsed.

A sickening ripple moved beneath his shirt before the fabric split along the seams. Dark, chitinous ridges forced their way through skin, glossy and segmented, catching the light like polished armor. His shoulder blades bulged outward, stretching, tearing, reforming into angular protrusions that twitched as though searching for balance.

Cage screamed, but the sound fractured halfway through. His jaw elongated, snapping forward with a wet pop as mandibles forced their way through his cheeks. Bone reshaped itself with audible cracks. His nose flattened. His eyes widened, then fractured into multifaceted planes that shimmered like fractured glass.

Their legs bent backward at the knees.

The transformation was not clean. It was violent geometry. Muscles rethreaded themselves. Skin hardened into layered plates of dark green and sand-colored exoskeleton. Veins darkened and sank beneath translucent segments. Fingers fused, splitting into clawed digits tipped with hooked barbs.

Their breathing changed.

It became a rasping, clicking rhythm, mechanical and insectile.

When Byron lifted his head, the human in him was gone. What remained was something tall and angular, half upright but never fully human again. A humanoid frame wrapped in locust armor. Segmented abdomen flexing. Jagged wings, not yet fully formed, twitching against torn fabric.

Cage rose beside him, movements too sharp, too precise. His head tilted with unsettling, predatory calculation. Mandibles flexed. A dry, chittering sound escaped him.

The war had taken two men.

It had returned two predators.

***

Petros, watching magically through Byrons' eyes smiled as he finally saw the mighty red dragon, the creature who would help him fulfill his destiny.

***

The things they were made into by Petros over three thousand and five hundred years before, stared hungrily at Aragon.

Aragon's anger grew, not like a flare, but like a furnace being fed.

The young man could no longer contain the beast.

It began in his chest. A low vibration, deep and resonant, as though something massive had awakened behind his ribs. His breath thickened. Heat rolled off him in waves, distorting the air. The ground beneath his torn sneakers/dragon feet darkened, stone cracking under pressure that had nothing to do with weight alone.

As he moved toward the pair, Aragon continued to grow.

Muscle thickened along his arms and back, straining against flesh that could no longer pretend to be human. His spine arched and elongated, vertebrae stacking and reshaping with grinding, tectonic force. His neck stretched forward, lengthening in increments which seemed impossible, each movement accompanied by the ripple of expanding red scales, countless,

107

endless, flowing across his skin like molten armor cooling into permanence.

His shoulders split outward.

Wings tore free in full expansion, not the restrained extensions of a hybrid form but vast, cathedral-sized structures of sinew and scale. Membranes unfurled with a violent snap, stretching wide enough to swallow light. The wind recoiled from them.

His hands were no longer hands.

Claws erupted from his fingers, thick and curved, each one the length of a blade. Tendons rewired themselves visibly beneath scale and sinew, locking into new, brutal connections meant for crushing and rending rather than grasping.

His jaw widened.

Teeth multiplied.

The last trace of his human face dissolved as his skull reshaped, pushing forward into a predatory snout lined with serrated ridges. Fire pulsed behind his eyes, glowing through slitted pupils that narrowed with lethal focus.

Protrusions surged from the left side, the right, and the crown of his head, jagged horns and ridges rising like a crown forged in war. They caught the light like living embers, framing him in a silhouette that looked less like a creature...and more like the embodiment of flame itself.

His torso thickened. His abdomen lengthened. His tail tore through the air behind him, sweeping wide, cracking stone as it struck the ground.

The hybrid was gone.

What stood before Byron and Cage was no longer a teen wrestling with power.

It was a dragon, vast, ancient, and certain of its own fire. The beast stood twenty feet upward and sixty feet in width.

His wings snapped outward instinctively and presented with a wingspan of one hundred and twenty feet.

The transformation from young man to beast seemed to ignore all the scientific laws regarding the conservation of mass. And when Aragon inhaled, the world seemed to hold its breath with him

He roared majestically.

Byron hissed as he materialized and withdrew a sword with Cage doing the same thing.

"We take the head, "started Byron, his voice now raspy, "we can be done with this quickly, Petros will let us consume the caucus."

"Alright," agreed Cage also with a raspy voice. "I'll distract him, you get the head!"

Byron looked at Cage with contempt.

Cage ran and futtered in flight towards Aragon, confident and certain he could hurt the beast, like he had done so many times before with other hybrids.

"Argh!" yelled cage as he moved blindly towards Aragon.

Aragon jumped up and then landed on Cage, left claw first, knocking the sword off to the side.

He then lifted his claw off of Cage, who twitched as he tried to get himself up when without warning a swift blue flame hit Cage, disintegrating him where he lay.

Aragon then looked from the charred ground over to Byron who moved swiftly towards him with the sword."

Aragon appeared to inhale slowly

Byron remembered, *inhale comes before flame throw*.

Aragon shot the flame out and Byron leapt over the flame and towards Aragon.

Byron then jabbed the sword into Aragon's shoulder, causing the dragon to wince briefly.

"You're done!" proclaimed Byron just as the dragon reached down and grabbed Byron's elongated legs with his teeth, causing the locust looking creature to scream.

Aragon then threw him upward and then bit him in half, causing the top half of Byron's body to fall to the ground and then he spat the other half of his enemy out. He then disintegrated both halves of the locust looking creature with the blue flame.

Looking around and satisfied that he didn't see anyone else attempting to take him down, Aragon ignored the camera flashes as he roared and as his majestic wings assisted him with rising up.

FALAP.

FALAP

FALAP.

FALAP.

Aragon took to the sky and flew quickly back to where he left Tyler.

As the dragon approached Tyler, passers-by who were attempting first aide on him scurried back out of the way.

And as the dragon started lowering himself, he morphed slowly back into human/hybrid form with his wings extended, face partially humanoid with dragon scale covering.

Gawkers looked on but his features remained blurry to them as some folk rubbed their eyes in confusion.

Aragon quickly and carefully scooped up Tyler who was now bleeding profusely and not moving.

FALAP.

FALAP.

Aragon, with Tyler Landon in his arms, took off towards the sky.

***

As dusk started to settle over Banner University Medical Center, the emergency department actually seemed pretty calm and quiet.

Doctor Maya Gardon just finished signing off on a couple of charts when she decided to call home and check on her son.

She listened for the phone ringing and then -

"Yo this is AJ, leave your incidentals."

BEEP-

"What use is it for me to pay a cell phone bill for you if you never answer your phone," she paused and let out a sigh. "Call me back when you get this message."

She hung up the phone as she heard a commotion at the entrance bay for the emergency vehicles."

She quickly made her way through the crowd. "What have we got?"

A nurse shouted, "teenage male with multiple stab wounds, no active bleeding, multiple lacerations, semi-conscious."

As she reached the gurney, she saw another teenager standing next to the gurney, crying.

"Mom, you've got to help him!" cried Aaron.

14

THE MONITOR BEEPED steadily.

Tyler's private hospital room was too bright for what had brought him there.

The overhead lights cast a steady, artificial glow over white walls and polished floors, as if cleanliness alone could erase the violence that had delivered him through the emergency doors.

The blinds were drawn halfway, muting the outside world into indistinct shadows.

The bed sat centered in the room, crisp sheets tucked with clinical precision around a body that looked too small against them.

An IV line threaded into Tyler's right forearm.

A monitor pulsed beside him, its green waveform steady and indifferent. Each beep echoed slightly in the otherwise hushed room, the sound both reassuring and accusatory, life measured in numbers.

There were no visible signs of what had truly happened.

No scorch marks. No shattered windows. No wings.

But something felt unsettling.

The air carried the sterile scent of antiseptic, yet beneath it lingered the faintest trace of ozone, subtle, nearly imperceptible, as if electricity had once passed too close to flesh.

On the bedside table sat his glasses, placed carefully by a nurse who had no idea that the boy wearing them had been carried through the sky.

A private room. A courtesy extended because of his age. Quiet. Controlled.

But outside those walls, something dangerous had occurred.

And the hospital, for all its machines and protocols, had not been built for that.

Tyler's mother stood near the bed with the composure of a woman accustomed to crisis, but this was different.

She had already read the chart twice. Spoken to the attending physician in clipped, professional tones. There were bruises. Mild trauma. Nothing that explained the way he had been found, or how he had arrived.

Her dark hair, streaked now with deliberate threads of silver, was pulled back tightly, though a few strands had escaped near her temples. She looked younger in her work gear than she felt in that moment.

But standing beside Tyler, her hands hovered uncertainly over his, unsure what she could do for her baby at this moment.

Her voice softened when she spoke to him.

"Tyler... sweetheart..."

The words carried strength, and fear carefully hidden beneath it.

But beneath the tough and calm exterior, was a mother who had already lost too much sleep over one small, fragile boy who had once needed help tying his shoes.

His father stood at the foot of the bed, arms folded tight, eyes fixed on Tyler's face like he was afraid it might vanish if he looked away.

Tyler's father stood at the foot of the bed at first, as though unsure how close he was allowed to get.

He had aged into his strength. Broad shoulders still solid, hair thinning at the temples but stubbornly dark in places. His work, long hours, steady and physical, had carved endurance into him rather than fragility.

He didn't understand what had happened.

He had heard only fragments:

"Found unconscious."

"No witnesses."

"Unusual transport."

He watched the machines more than the doctors. He watched the rise and fall of Tyler's chest. He memorized the rhythm of the monitor's beeps.

When he finally moved closer, his large hand wrapped around Tyler's smaller one, careful, as if afraid pressure alone might break something unseen.

He didn't speak much.

But there was something in his eyes, something between anger and awe.

Because somewhere inside him, he knew.

This had not been an accident.

And whatever had brought his son here... might come again.

They knew he was medically stable, but that didn't make this any easier.

The television mounted in the corner of the room played softly, volume low but impossible to ignore.

"...authorities are still attempting to piece together the events surrounding the reported kidnapping of a teenage boy earlier today..."

Tyler's mother glanced at the screen.

Security footage. Blurry stills. A black sedan.

"...the victim was later found unconscious near the edge of the desert..."

Her breath caught.

"...witnesses in the area reported what they described as a 'large red dragon-like figure' engaged in a violent altercation with what appeared to be two massive insectoid creatures..."

She scoffed softly, shaking her head. "That's ridiculous."

But her hands were trembling.

"...officials have not confirmed these accounts..."

She turned the TV off.

Silence rushed in to fill the space.

Aaron stood near the door, shoulders hunched, hands clasped so tightly his knuckles had gone white. He hadn't sat down. Hadn't spoken. He just stood there like a kid waiting to be punished.

Tyler's mother looked at him.

"Thank you," she said quietly. "For staying."

Aaron nodded. "I wasn't gonna leave."

Aaron's mother, standing near her son, gave Tyler's mother a small nod and touched him gently as she left the room, signaling him to come with her.

Aaron studied Tyler for a moment longer than necessary and then followed his mother into the hallway.

Maya then reached up and pulled the blinds closed from the hallway, affording the Landon family some privacy.

"Come with me," Maya said.

Aaron's stomach dropped.

He followed her down the hall, past the nurses' stations and quiet rooms, to a small conference room tucked away from the chaos.

She closed the door.

And locked it.

Then she turned to face him.

"This room is soundproof," she said evenly. "We use it for family meetings, to deliver bad news..." she sighed.

Aaron swallowed.

She crossed her arms. "Now I'm going to ask you something, and I need you to understand this clearly."

Her eyes locked onto his.

"I am not asking as just your mother," she said. "I am asking as a physician and as someone who cares about helping to protect you boys as much as possible, but in order to do that, I need you to tell me the truth."

Aaron flinched.

"What happened?" she asked.

He shook his head immediately. "You wouldn't believe me."

"Try me."

Silence stretched.

The tele monitors from down the hall seemed impossibly loud now.

Aaron exhaled.

Then he told her.

Not carefully. Not strategically.

He told her about the dreams, the dragon. About training in the desert. About the sorceress. About being hunted by a four thousand year old man. About Tyler being taken because of him.

He told her about the rage.

About the fire.

About the men who weren't men.

He told her everything.

When he finished, his voice was hoarse and his eyes were wet.

His mother didn't interrupt once.

She just listened.

When he finally stopped, she sat down slowly in one of the chairs.

"You're telling me," she said choosing her words carefully, "that my son is a dragon who was being trained by a sorceress, who is being hunted by a man or something, who is at least four thousand years old?"

Aaron nodded.

"Someone is hunting you."

"Yes."

"And Tyler was hurt because he stood with you and was helping you?"

Aaron broke then.

"I never meant for him to get hurt," he said, voice cracking. "I tried to keep him out of it. I swear."

She closed her eyes for a long moment.

Then opened them.

"Tyler is alive," she said. "That matters. But you need to give me one good reason I should believe a word of what you're saying."

RIP.

Aarons' wings tore out the back of his jacket.

Dr. Maya Gardon looked from the wings to her sixteen-year-old son, and fainted.

***

"Mom!" yelled Aaron as he tapped his mom lightly on the face. "Mom!"

She stirred as he started to assist her to a sitting position. "Easy mom," he started as she looked around and noticed she was still in the conference room. She was hoping she had been having a little nightmare.

She leaned forward. "Aaron, what you're going through, the things you're describing, they don't just end, not on their own."

"I know," he whispered. "And I'm afraid my journey is just starting."

She nodded slowly, doctor-brain already working, already cataloging risk.

"Then we're going to have to be very careful," she said.

Aaron looked up sharply. "You're... not calling anyone?"

"No," she said. "There's no one for me to call. But you don't get to carry this alone anymore."

She stood and unlocked the door.

They stepped back into the hallway and headed back towards Tyler's room, where his parents were getting comfortable by his side, as he continued his sleep.

"You've managed to keep yourself safe this far," she started. "Your fathers' family history I know very little of, the things you're learning from this sorceress, I definitely can't teach you, but I will always be by your side and support you anyway I can."

A tear came out of Aaron's eye.

"Whatever help you need on this journey, in any way I can support you, you let me know."

Aaron looked over at Tyler. "If you don't mind, you know since you're always here at the hospital and all, do you mind keepin' an eye on him?" he asked, gesturing to Tyler.

"Not at all," said Maya.

15

PETROS HATED WAITING. He stood at the edge of the obsidian chamber, hands clasped behind his back, staring into the fish tank.

Across the room, news footage played over and over again, desert roads, emergency lights, humans pointing at the sky.

Two men who turned into large insect type creatures.

A large red dragon that killed them after being attacked by them.

The pictures and videos were blurry and incomplete.

But undeniable to anyone looking at them.

He now stood alone, after four thousand years, he was alone. He could probably call someone from the Trilateral Commission and procure a couple of henchmen, with whom he could envibe with some of his mojo to take out the dragon, but anyone he could get would not be as well practiced as Byron and Cage.

For thirty-five hundred years, they helped him corner the human / dragon hybrids and they learned how to improve and adapt with each dragon's skill and increase in strength, yet some invisible kid just takes them out after his second encounter against them?

Might be better if I just take him out myself, thought Petros.

"So," Petros said softly to no one at all. "You reek of raw power. The sky torn open by wings that did not yet understand restraint."

He paused as he added fish food into the tank.

"Rage suits you," he continued. "As does control."

He turned away from the tank / mirror, robe whispering against the stone floor.

"But rage is crude," Petros continued, his voice tightening. "And your control can be influenced."

He flexed his fingers.

"I wonder with my hunters gone, will you still run and hide?"

Petros smiled thinly.

"I guess we will see."

He raised one hand and the lighting from the fishtank darkened.

"You will come to me," he whispered. "Not because I chase you... but because you will realize fury is not enough."

***

The desert was quiet.

Not training quiet. Not ritual quiet.

Just still.

Aaron sat on a rock across from Sorrie, elbows on his knees, hands clasped together. The sand beneath him was cool this morning, the air thin and sharp.

Sorrie studied him for a long moment before speaking.

122

"You lost control," she said.

Aaron didn't argue. "Yeah."

"You didn't listen," she continued. "You didn't wait. You didn't think."

"I know."

Sorrie narrowed her eyes. "And yet you survived."

Aaron looked up at her. "And Tyler has a chance to survive also."

"You didn't survive because of your rage," she said flatly. "That was strength."

Aaron nodded slowly. "I believe you."

That surprised her.

"You do?" she asked.

"Yeah," he said as he had tossed a pebble he had been playing with into the sand. "Because if rage was enough...Petros would've been dead a long time ago."

Sorrie's expression didn't change, but something in her posture softened.

"You looked powerful," she said.

"I felt powerful," Aaron admitted. "Terrifyingly powerful."

"And?"

"And it scared me," he said honestly. "Not them. Me."

Sorrie waited.

"My mom knows now," Aaron said quietly.

That got her attention.

"She didn't freak," he continued. "She didn't run. She didn't call anyone. She believed me."

Sorrie exhaled slowly. "That changes things."

"It does," Aaron agreed. "Tyler's stable. He's gonna wake up. And now I know, really know, what my dragon side can do if I maintain control."

He clenched his fist, then relaxed it.

"I don't want to be he who loses himself inside of himself," he said. "I don't want to win by losing myself."

Sorrie studied him carefully. "Petros will not fall to anger; he actually relishes within it."

"I know," Aaron said. "And that was me lashing out, not fighting."

"And yet," she said, "you believe you can contain it now?"

Aaron looked out across the desert.

"I do," he said. "Because now I know what happens if I don't."

He stood.

He ran straight for the edge of the cliff and did a swan dive over as Sorrie stared.

A moment later, from where he dove, the dragon shot straight up into the sky.

FALAP.

FALAP.

He circled the air in proud majestic glides and then-

FALAP.

FALAP.

He soon returned to the cliff and with nothing more than a mere thought, instantly morphed into his human form as he landed and walked back towards Sorrie.

"I'm not afraid of my dragon side anymore," Aaron continued. "I respect it. And I know now it's something I have to protect not unleash."

Sorrie smiled faintly.

"Good," she said. "Because Petros is waiting for you to make that mistake again."

Aaron met her gaze.

"Then he's gonna be disappointed."

16

TYLER OPENED HIS eyes slowly as he looked around the hospital room.

He saw a female doctor looking at him smiling.

"Good Morning," started Dr. Gardon, "I'm Dr. Maya Gardon, You're here at Banner Medical Center due to a recent chain of events which included your kidnapping and attempted murder. Can you tell me your name and date of birth?"

"Tyler Ishkabibbel Landon, Five Seventeen," he grunted, "eighty-nine!"

"Good...and where are you now?"

"You just said Banner Medical Center?"

"That is good!" she said as she closed his chart. "Your parents are in the cafeteria getting breakfast." She moved closer to him. "I am Aaron's mother."

"Which Aaron?" he asked testing.

She smiled. "Let me rephrase myself, I am Aragon's mother"!

Tyler stiffened.

"Relax," she said, "I don't turn into a dragon, and Aaron told me everything, including if you hadn't helped him, he doesn't think he'd be alive right now."

Tyler smiled. "He said that?"

"He most certainly did, "replied Maya."

"Now I know he owes me," replied Tyler rubbing his hands together.

"By the way," started Maya, "He brought you into us."

"Well that was incredibly kind of him."

Maya laughed. "I can see why he cares about you so much!"

Tyler snapped his fingers. "By the way……Doctor…mom…I want to talk to you about Aaron's wardrobe."

She just looked at him smilingly while shaking her head in disbelief.

***

Aaron stood alone at the edge of the desert plateau, phone pressed to his ear, the wind tugging gently at his jacket vest.

He hadn't realized how tightly he'd been holding his breath until his mother spoke.

"He's stable," Maya said. "Conscious. Talking. Being himself."

Aaron closed his eyes.

"Thank God," he whispered.

"He's asking questions," she continued. "Smart ones. And he remembers enough to know he was taken, but not enough to know *how* he got away."

Aaron nodded, even though she couldn't see him.

"That's good," he said. "That's really good."

"I wanted you to hear it from me first," Maya added. "And Aaron…"

"I know," he said gently. "I know."

They said their goodbyes.

Aaron lowered the phone slowly.

Sorrie was seated high on a sun-warmed rock when Aaron returned, watching the horizon like it might blink first.

"He's awake," Aaron said.

She looked up sharply.

"Stable," he continued. "Talking. Cracking jokes."

Sorrie exhaled, a long, controlled release of tension she hadn't allowed herself until now.

"Good," she said. "Now he stays safe, and out of the way."

Aaron nodded. "And I don't want Petros getting a second shot."

Sorrie studied him. "You're thinking ahead."

"I have to," Aaron replied. "Tyler's human. He doesn't regenerate. And Petros already used him once."

She rose to her feet.

"So we remove him from the board," she said.

Aaron shook his head. "And we start keeping our eye on Petros."

That made her pause.

"Petros still can't see me unless I let the dragon surface," Aaron continued. "He can't track me in human form. But Tyler?" He hesitated. "Tyler's visible, and he's stationary, currently of no use to Petros"

Sorrie's eyes narrowed, not in disagreement, but realization.

"So he's..." she said carefully.

"Safe," Aaron interjected. "no longer a worry."

She considered this.

"Petros watches patterns," Sorrie said slowly. "Movement. Proximity. Reaction."

"And because he has nothing to watch and likely assumes, no one is watching him," Aaron added. "He will make a mistake."

A corner of her mouth twitched.

"He does seem arrogant," she admitted.

"I am bound to learn something that will make him tick," Aaron continued, "then I bait him for the final fight."

Sorrie looked out over the desert again.

"You know...This only works if you stay disciplined," she said. "No rage."

"I know," Aaron said. "That's why it'll work."

She met his gaze.

"You're trying to protect Tyler by risking yourself," she said.

Aaron didn't hesitate. "I already am."

Sorrie nodded once.

"Then we do things your way, "she said. "Flip the script!"

17

TYLER HATED HOSPITAL ceilings.

They were too white. Too honest. Too bright for someone who'd just been stabbed three times and thrown out of a moving car.

He adjusted slightly in the bed, wincing.

He looked down at the areas where his dressings sat just under his checker patterned hospital gown, feeling the Dankins-soaked gauze packing covered by the ABD pads and medipore tape, almost forgetting the dressings were there until he had to move.

Then the pain would snap him back to reality.

The door to his hospital room clicked open softly.

Aaron walked inside, looking at his young friend sitting on the bed wearing the hospital gown.

He didn't speak immediately.

Tyler didn't look at him right away either.

For a moment, they just existed in the same room.

"You look like trash," Tyler muttered finally.

Aaron smirked faintly. "You look worse."

"Fair enough."

Silence again.

"Locust people?" asked Tyler.

"How'd you..."

Tylers' voice went up an octave like it usually did when he got excited, "Dude it's been all over the news...giant locust people killed by fire breathing Aragon!"

"Fire breathing Aragon?" asked Aaron.

"Well, I added that last part!"

"Go figure."

Tyler laughed. "Ooh..."

"How you feelin?"

"Hurts like a sum-a-bitch," Tyler said, while guarding his abdomen.

"Well, you were brave."

"What'd I do, besides become a victim," started Tyler dolefully, "and almost jeopardized the mission."

Aaron sat down in the recliner next to the hospital bed. "You didn't jeopardize anything!"

"What ev's," started Tyler. "So tell me...did Petros start monologuing before you smelted him?"

Aaron stared at Tyler with a long pause. "Petros wasn't there."

"Wait...what?" asked Tyler. "You were in full fiery dragon mode and he didn't show up to...you know."

"I don't know," started Aaron, "maybe I caught him off guard, but he wasn't there."

Tyler looked at Aaron with the *I can't believe you missed the sign*' look. "The dude waited four thousand years to take your head off and he doesn't show up for his big finale. Dude, you scared the shit out of him."

"C'mon Tyler be serious."

"I am," argued Tyler. "He literally trained for four thousand years to gut you and a sixteen-year-old kid scares him off?"

"Never thought of it like that," said Aaron.

"Well I'm takin' notes," replied Tyler.

"Well it's a good thing he didn't show up."

"Yeah, cause you would've roasted him."

"No," started Aaron, "because I lost control."

"You could have totally beat him like that," said Tyler.

"That's the false sense of security he wants me to have," started Aaron. "It's what the Sorceress has been warning me about."

Tyler studied him now.

The dragon wasn't surfacing.

It wasn't flickering in Aaron's eyes.

It was... contained.

"You figured it out," Tyler said.

Aaron exhaled through his nose. "Yeah."

"Petros wanted you angry."

"And he wanted me predictable," Aaron added.

Tyler smiled faintly. "Same thing."

Aaron got up from the chair.

"In any case, I can't beat him by reacting," Aaron said. "I have to make him react, so that I can beat him."

Tyler's brow lifted.

"And how exactly do you plan on doing that?"

Aaron hesitated.

"By somehow infiltrating him."

Tyler blinked.

"How are you supposed to do that?"

Aaron walked closer.

"With your help!"

"I didn't volunteer for that," started Tyler, "He tried to kill me!"

"I know."

Aaron's voice then softened.

"But this time you will stay out of harm's way."

Tyler looked away.

"So I'm not really gonna help you," he muttered. "I know...I'm a liability."

Aaron shook his head.

"No," he said firmly. "That's not what I mean."

Tyler looked back at him.

"You didn't panic," Aaron continued. "You didn't break. You told me to go keep going."

Tyler swallowed.

"I thought I was dying."

"And you still thought about stopping them, to save me."

Tyler's fingers tightened slightly around the blanket.

Aaron leaned forward.

"From the moment you found out about me, about Aragon," Aaron started. "You've done nothing but try to help me and hype me up...heck, you even named me."

Tyler's eyes sharpened now.

"So what are you saying?"

Aaron didn't hesitate.

"I need you," started Aaron, "I am not the tech wiz you are and I definitely wouldn't have gotten as far as I had without you, so, I need you to help me see this through."

The words hung there.

For the first time in this journey, Tyler wasn't being described as the someone who had to be protected.

"Will you help me in my fight against Petros?" Aaron asked.

Tyler studied him carefully.

"I don't breathe fire or fly or throw boulders with muscular clawed...hands or whatever they are," he said.

"No," Aaron agreed. "You think."

Tyler almost laughed but didn't.

"You're serious."

"Completely."

Tyler stared at the ceiling again.

Then back at Aaron.

"So what's my role in this grand dragon strategy?"

Aaron's voice lowered.

"You stay exactly who you are."

Tyler frowned. "That's it?"

"That's it."

Silence filled the room again.

Then Tyler smirked slightly.

"You know," he said, "I always thought I'd go out in some big blaze of glory."

Aaron raised an eyebrow.

"Turns out," Tyler continued, "I'm more useful alive and annoying."

Aaron's smile widened slightly.

"Well, I was talking about your computer skills and your ability to get information, but yeah, the alive and annoying thing works well too!"

Tyler's tone shifted.

"I will help you," he said quietly. "But no pun intended, I am grounded so long as I'm in the hospital."

Aaron nodded once.

"Well, I am at your mercy with that, I know but it's something.

Aaron went still.

"Oh by the way," started Aaron. "Sorrie sends her love."

Tyler's voice sharpened.

"Wait...did she say that? Or did she just say something like...get better twirp."

Aaron laughed.

"C'mon bro, don't leave me hangin'!"

Aaron's expression changed.

"Try not to get stuck in a mirror dimension trying to figure it out," Aaron added.

"Are those real? Awe man!"

Aaron just laughed.

"By the way," started Tyler, "I had a word with Doctor Gardon 'bout your wardrobe."

They shared a look.

Then they both laughed.

"Serious though," started Tyler, "She said she sends me her love?"

18

TYLER WAS SITTING upright now. It was not the time to slouch when a doctor was in the room.

He was bruised.

He felt stiff.

But he still sat fully upright.

Aaron stood near the window when he entered, hands in his jacket pockets, dragon quiet beneath his skin.

Maya was already there, seated beside Tyler's bed, reviewing something on a tablet.

She looked up first.

"You're early," she said. "I wasn't expecting you to be here."

Aaron shrugged slightly. "Couldn't sit still."

Tyler smirked. "He's been pacing."

"I don't pace."

"You absolutely do pace," said Maya.

Maya stood. "I'm going to check on a couple of labs. Five minutes."

She stepped out, closing the door softly behind her.

Silence settled.

Tyler studied Aaron for a moment.

"You look calmer."

"I am."

"Good. Because that whole 'ten-foot dragon biting people in half' thing? Bit dramatic."

Aaron winced slightly. "They weren't people at that point, already gone."

"I know."

A beat.

"And now he's blind," offered Aaron.

"Petros?"

Aaron nodded yes.

"How do you know?"

"His goons are gone!"

"You think he only has two?" asked Tyler.

"He hasn't sent anyone else looking for us."

"You sure about that?"

"For now," started Aaron, "yes."

Tyler shifted carefully against the pillows.

"So, I get out of the hospital somehow," started Tyler. "Then what's the plan?"

Aaron leaned against the wall.

"I learn what I can about him, then I bait him."

Tyler raised an eyebrow. "With what?"

"Still trying to figure that part out.'

Tyler considered that.

"Until then, you disappear."

"Remember, he already can't see me."

"And what if he comes after me?"

Aaron nodded. "I don't think he will."

Tyler smirked faintly.

"You can't guarantee that."

Aaron exhaled. "

"No, but my back up for that is to have sorceress create a phantom trail of you moving around the hospital. Petros will still sense you're here even after you leave, but he will never be able to find you..."

"...because I won't be here," interrupted Tyler.

As Aaron stared at him, Tyler blinked slowly.

"You're looking at the wrong guy," Tyler said.

"No," Aaron said firmly. "I'm not."

Tyler's brow lifted.

Aaron stepped closer.

"I think you notice things I don't."

Tyler studied him carefully.

"You really believe that."

"Yeah."

Tyler looked down at his blanket covered legs. "Okay," he relented.

"Okay?" Aaron asked confirming.

"Okay," Tyler repeated. "I'm in."

A quiet knock didn't come.

Instead—

A throat cleared from the doorway.

Both boys froze.

Aaron turned slowly.

Tyler's parents stood in the hall.

His father's arms folded.

His mother's expression unreadable.

They had heard enough.

Not everything.

But enough.

The room went very still.

Aaron's pulse ticked once hard in his neck.

Tyler's father stepped fully into the room.

"Dragon?" he asked calmly.

No one spoke.

Maya reappeared behind them in the hallway, stopping mid-step.

Tyler looked at Aaron.

Aaron looked at Tyler.

And neither of them ran.

19

THE ROOM FELT different now. Less like a hospital room and more like an interrogation room.

There would be no more pretending.

There would be no more brushing anything aside.

Tyler's mother sat slowly in the chair near the window.

His father remained standing, hands-on hips.

Maya closed the door carefully.

"Why don't I start with this simple question," Tyler's mother said. "That whole dragon sighting incident on the news...was that real?"

Silence.

Aaron didn't look away as Tyler looked up at him.

"Yes."

Her eyes widened slightly.

"Okay, so there really is a dragon," she said calmly.

"Is the dragon...your pet," she asked.

"No maam," Aaron replied.

She clutched her chest. "Oh thank God!"

Aaron looked at his mother, Maya looked at Tyler, and Tyler looked worriedly at Aaron.

"Were you both in the same area where the dragon was seen?"

"Yes, ma'am."

Tyler's father rubbed his chin slowly.

"And the insect monsters?"

"Also real," Tyler muttered.

"Yes they were two men at first and then they changed into the giant locusts," offered Aaron. "But the dragon...that was me."

"I thought you said you didn't have a dragon?" asked Mrs. Landon.

"I don't have a dragon Mrs. Landon," started Aaron. "I am the dragon!"

Aaron then held up his hands and morphed them into the mighty arms from the forearms down.

The Landons then looked at each other.

Mrs. Landon turned and faced Maya.

"Are you a dragon too?"

"No," started Maya. "He gets that from his father's side of the family. I just recently found out about this myself."

His father nodded once, like he was accepting a weather report.

"Okay," said Tylers' father.

Tyler blinked.

"Okay?"

His father looked at him. "Son, we watched the news. We saw the footage."

"Does that mean you..."

"We may not understand it," his father interrupted, "but we know what we saw."

Tyler's mother looked at Aaron.

"You saved him."

Aaron hesitated.

"Yes."

She exhaled slowly. "Thank you."

Aaron nodded respectfully. "In all fairness, he saved me first."

Tyler's father stepped forward slightly.

"So," he said carefully, "this Petros guy is gunning for you."

Aaron stiffened.

"You're hunting him?"

"I'm not hunting him," Aaron corrected. "I'm...we're trying to stop him."

His father nodded thoughtfully.

"And Tyler is..."

He searched for the word.

"Your tech kick?"

Aaron blinked.

Tyler stared at him.

"My what?" Aaron asked.

Tyler's father frowned slightly. "You know. Like the guy in the chair. The computer brain. The backup."

Aaron and Tyler slowly turned toward each other.

Shock.

Recognition.

Tyler pointed weakly at his father.

"That," he said. "That's exactly what I said."

Aaron stared at him. "You did."

Tyler's father looked between them. "Well, I didn't mean to coin a phrase."

Tyler smirked. "No, no. We got it."

His father nodded once.

"Okay. Then we'll help."

Aaron shook his head immediately. "No."

All eyes went to him.

"I am not putting Tyler in danger again."

Tyler's father lifted a hand calmly.

"Relax."

Aaron's jaw tightened.

"You won't," his father said. "He won't be in the field."

Tyler blinked. "Dad..."

"Basement," his father continued.

Everyone paused.

"Our basement," he clarified. "Secure. Wired. Tyler always does his techy stuff down there, I'm sure we can outfit it a little better so he can be of better help to you."

Tyler's mother nodded. "We have excellent internet service."

Maya raised an eyebrow. "Really?"

Tyler's father shrugged slightly. "I work for the C-I-A -my only child loves technology, why wouldn't my home have that as part of its foundation?"

He looked at Aaron.

"You want to watch this Petros guy but don't know where to find him."

Aaron nodded slowly.

"That's where we come in."

Tyler straightened slightly in the bed.

His father continued.

"Satellite anomalies. News feeds. Power grid irregularities. You said he's ancient?"

"Yes."

"Then he's sloppy in modern systems," his father said. "People like that always are."

Aaron's eyes sharpened.

"You're saying we track disturbances."

"I'm saying," his father replied, "you don't fight a war blind, we start with those things, then we do a facial recognition search until you're able to identify him with certainty."

"What about keeping Tyler safe?" asked Aaron. "I don't want him being returned to school, just for him to become a target again."

"We can have Tyler finish out the school year at home," started Mrs. Landon. "We will get him a medical exclusion set up."

Maya crossed her arms, impressed.

Tyler looked at Aaron slowly.

Aaron looked back.

A smile tugged at both of them.

They were not being cocky.

They were not going to be reckless.

They were going to get ready.

Tyler's father clapped his hands once.

"Alright then," he said. "We help. Safely."

Aaron hesitated only a second.

Then nodded.

"Okay."

Tyler leaned back against the pillow.

"So," he said lightly. "Guess we've got a secret H - Q- now."

Aaron smirked.

"Guess we do."

20

THE BASEMENT still smelled like old cardboard and laundry detergent.

It had been used mostly for storage. Seasonal decorations. A treadmill no one used. Boxes labeled *COLLEGE* and *TAXES* and *DO NOT THROW OUT*.

Now it was becoming something else.

Tyler sat in a rolling chair wrapped in a hospital blanket but no longer attached to an IV pole.

Mr. Landon moved around him like a man on a mission, lifting panels, dragging extension cords, setting up tables with the confidence of someone who had built workspaces out of nothing before.

"Okay," Tyler's father said, wiping his hands. "Power first. Redundancy second. Signal last."

Tyler raised an eyebrow. "You've done this before."

His father didn't look up. "I've done a lot of things before."

A folding table became a command surface. A second table held monitors. A third held what looked like a half-disassembled router, a soldering kit, and a laptop which already had multiple windows open.

Tyler pointed weakly. "That one needs to be closer."

His father slid it without complaint.

Mrs. Landon watched from the stairs, arms folded.

"Please tell me you're not turning the basement into a military installation," she said.

Tyler's father glanced up. "It's not military."

Tyler chimed in. "It's tactical."

Mrs. Landon sighed. "That's worse."

Aaron stood at the bottom of the stairs, quiet. Observing. Still adjusting to the fact their parents all now knew about Aragon, or him.

Tyler's father stepped toward him holding something small and dark in his palm.

"Open your ear."

Aaron blinked. "What?"

Tyler leaned forward. "It's an earpiece. But not the normal kind."

Aaron hesitated, then leaned slightly.

Tyler's father carefully placed it in Aaron's ear. It seated itself with a soft suction fit, almost like it locked.

Aaron lifted a hand. "It's... stuck."

"Correct," Tyler said.

Aaron frowned. "How do I take it out?"

"You don't," Tyler replied.

Aaron's eyes widened. "Ty..."

Tyler held up a finger. "Hear me out. You morph, your body changes. Everything shifts. Clothes tear. Gear falls off, and yes you're able to magically repair them, but this is different."

Tyler's father finished the thought. "So we grabbed something that stays throughout your changes. Medical-grade suction seal. Flexible composite. It sits deep enough to hold but not deep enough to harm."

Aaron tested it again. It didn't budge.

Tyler grinned. "Congratulations. You're Bluetooth-enabled!"

Mrs. Landon muttered, "I'm going to pretend I didn't hear that sentence."

Aaron blinked hard. "So you'll... be in my head?"

Tyler shook his head. "Not your head. Your ear. I don't want to know your thoughts. That's disturbing."

Aaron's mouth twitched.

"What about when I need to shower? Get my ears cleaned? Or go to the doctor?"

Mr. Landon handed what looked like a small screwdriver to Aaron.

"Relax Aaron. You can remove and install the earpiece at any time. It's just meant for you and Tyler to have radio contact at all times.

"Okay cool," smiled Aaron.

"...and so he can see what you see," added Mr. Landon.

"Wait...what?" asked Tyler.

Tyler's father tapped the monitor, bringing up a clean audio panel.

"You're not alone anymore," he said calmly. "That's the whole point."

Aaron stared at the screen, maps, feeds, data.

"Who are you people?" asked Aaron.

"I told you I'm with the C-I-A," answered Mr. Landon. "Covert ops, planning and implementation...but don't worry, you're not in our data base, and I will keep it that way."

Aaron nodded once and smiled.

"Okay."

"Unless Tyler gets hurt again," added Mr. Landon.

Aaron just looked at him as Tyler chuckled.

***

The sun was beaming down in the desert again and it was quiet.

Not peaceful.

Just ready, as if awaiting some great presence or happening.

Aaron stood on the plateau while Sorrie circled him like an instructor and a predator at the same time.

"You are distracted," she said.

Aaron kept his eyes forward. "I'm listening."

Sorrie's mouth twitched. "If I'm not the only one you are listening to, it is still a distraction."

In Aaron's ear, Tyler's voice crackled faintly.

"Tell her you're multitasking."

Aaron didn't smile.

Sorrie stopped. "Tell Tyler I can hear him."

"What...really?" Tyler queried.

"Tyler, not now," Aaron replied.

"Oh my bad," Tyler whispered. "I forgot you're in mystical dragon boot camp."

Sorrie narrowed her eyes. "Ask Tyler if he would like three matching scars on the other side?"

Aaron exhaled. "Ouch."

"That was more him than you?" she asked sharply.

"Yes."

"Good," Sorrie said. "Let's get started!"

Tyler's voice came through again, quieter now. Less joking.

"Tell her I'm an asset."

Aaron swallowed.

"No he is not an asset," started Sorrie, "but you are Aragon's friend, so I will ask you, keep your rambling to a minimum."

"Yes maam," relented Tyler.

Sorrie lifted her hand.

The air pressure shifted.

"Again," she commanded.

Aaron ran.

He leapt.

He let the dragon surface, but not fully.

Just enough.

Scales flashed after morphing the skin. Heat shimmered at his shoulders.

Wings started to tear out of his back.

"Left side first!" Tyler barked in Aaron's ear.

Aaron reacted instantly, rolling his shoulder, letting the left-wing tear free before the right, preventing the imbalance that had nearly sent him spiraling last time.

Sorrie's eyes widened slightly.

Aaron launched upward cleanly.

FALAP.

FALAP.

He corrected his angle mid-flight.

Tyler's voice came through again, breathless. "Yes! Okay, now bank right...right, your tail may be causing a drag."

Aragon adjusted.

Perfected.

Controlled.

Sorrie watched without speaking.

He flew in large concentric patterns, smiling as the wind caressed his face and embraced his body.

FALAP.

FALAP.

FALAP.

He then descended towards Sorrie.

When Aragon landed, dust curling around his feet, he was human again in seconds.

He inhaled once, steady.

Sorrie stepped closer.

"That was disciplined," she said quietly.

Aaron nodded. "It has to be, I can't afford any slip ups with him."

Tyler's voice softened. "You're getting good at this, man."

Aaron's throat tightened slightly. "Yeah, I think I am."

***

The printer in Tyler's basement hummed to life as a page started printing out.

Tyler yanked the page out and passed it to Aaron who took it and skimmed down.

"Donali Petros," started Tyler, "sounds like a Ninja Turtle...anyway...senior member of the Naples, Italy Chapter of the Trilateral Commission...he recently traveled from Italy and...whoa...dude bought a whole house just so he could be near you!"

"No need to be a dweeb Tyler! What's the Trilateral Commission?"

"I dunno and I'm just saying...bought a house? For something that was supposed to be a one and done?"

"Maybe he was gonna give it to his two...friends once he was done. I mean if he became a God, he'd no longer need to be here."

"Good point," started Tyler as he continued typing on the screen and you were right...Leslie Byron and Greg Cage, their names are also on the deed to the property."

Tyler then developed a mischievous look on his face.

He then just started typing while on the screen.

"I wonder...," started Tyler.

He paused.

"Oh, yeah, the submission for this paperwork is still new and processing, all funds have cleared...why don't we just have your rich uncle just leave the place to you."

"Tyler...what?" asked Aaron. "Don't even think about it!"

"Oh I'm thinking about it," said Tyler smilingly as he manipulated the files and put Aaron's name on there after removing Byron and Cage. "It's the least he can do since he's trying to decorate his room with your dragon head."

"Tyler I..."

Aarons' phone ringing intruded in on the conversation.

He pulled the phone out of his pocket, glanced at the screen, and flipped it open.

"Hey mom!"

He paused.

"Yeah I'm with Tyler now, he was just getting me the info I needed."

He paused again as he cupped the phone and mouthed to Tyler, *I'm serious T, don't do it!*

"Yeah I got it, burgers and fries out the deep freezer..."

"Already done," interrupted Tyler, "when Petros is gone, you'll be the youngest homeowner in Arizona."

Aaron looked from Tyler over to another area of the basement.

"Who knows what he's talkin' about mom," started Aaron, "I doubt even he knows!"

He paused as Tyler mocked him the background.

"Love you too mom, see you soon!"

He hung up the phone.

"Tyler!"

"What?" he asked. "I'm only looking out for your best interest!"

21

AS NIGHTTIME WELCOMED him with chirping crickets and a gentle breeze, he moved far away from the usual scenes, the school, Tyler's house, or even the desert plateau.

Aaron moved like a shadow.

He didn't bring rage.

He didn't bring fire.

He brought silence. He had to. Even though Petros could not see him, thanks to Sorrie's spell, other people could see him, so if Aaron brought too much attention to himself, that would almost certainly spell trouble.

Petros' sanctuary sat hidden the way old evil always tried to hide, stone and shadow and arrogance.

Aaron slipped inside while Petros was away, the air unnaturally still.

In his ear, Tyler whispered, "You sure this is smart?"

"No," Aaron whispered back. "But it's necessary."

He moved through the home looking at how neat and majestic everything seem on the inside, especially for it to be a simple rancher on the exterior.

153

"Wow," started Tyler as he could see everything Aaron was seeing. "This place is huge! You're going to thank me later."

"Yeah as I stare at my hefty estate tax bill, that will put me in debt...like forever."

"Don't sweat it dude," started Tyler. "Daddy Warbucks has very old money, I'm sure I'll be able to funnel some of that your way too."

"Well, it's all going to Aragon," started Aaron as he located a basement door.

"I thought you might say that my bad guy filleting amigo...I vote it be our base of operations..."

"You talk too much Tyler," interrupted Aaron.

Aaron made his way down the steps and into the obsidian chamber carefully.

"Wow," started Tyler, "this place is huge! I think your dragon form could fit down here."

Fish tank. Mirrors. Strange symbols. Old stone.

Aaron's pulse stayed low.

He placed a small device behind a carved ridge.

Then another under a stone lip near the fissure.

Then a third, tucked inside the base of the tank stand.

Tyler's father's voice came through for the first time, calm, controlled.

"Signal confirmed. You're live."

Aaron exhaled slowly.

"Thanks Mr. Landon."

Tyler whispered, "Bro... you are literally bugging an ancient bad guy."

Aaron's voice was barely audible. "Yes."

He finished.

He then slipped out as quietly as he entered.

***

The basement screens glowed like an artificial sunrise in the dark.

Tyler sat wrapped in a hoodie now, healing better, sharper again. His father sat beside him with a legal pad, writing down timestamps like this was a job.

Because it was.

His mother hovered occasionally, pretending she wasn't invested.

Aaron was back in the desert most days.

But his ear never left him.

Petros' sanctuary feed came through in fragments. Angles. Shadows. Audio more than video.

Hours passed.

Days.

Not much happened.

Petros moved around the chamber alone.

He spoke occasionally, but not to anyone.

To himself.

To the air.

To the idea of victory.

Tyler tapped his keyboard. "He's paranoid."

"He's alone," his father corrected. "That makes people talk."

"Or monsters," his mother muttered.

On the speaker, Petros' voice emerged, low, amused.

"...they always hide behind half-forms at first..."

Tyler leaned forward.

Petros continued, pacing.

"...the boy thinks he has control..."

Silence.

Then Petros laughed softly.

"...but every dragon has a true face."

Tyler's father's pen paused.

Petros' voice tightened, more focused now.

"I will make you show it," he whispered, almost tenderly. "I will take it from you."

Tyler's skin prickled.

His mother's expression hardened.

Tyler's father wrote the line down slowly.

Then looked at Tyler.

"That," he said quietly, "is motive beyond obsession."

Tyler swallowed.

"And that," he replied, "is what we're trying to avoid."

On the monitor, Petros stood still, staring into the dark glass of the fish tank like it was a mirror.

He smiled faintly.

As if he could feel the world watching.

As if he didn't care.

22

PETROS DID NOT believe in coincidence. Patterns meant interference. Silence meant intention. And intention meant opposition.

He stood before the obsidian tank, fingers hovering over the water's surface without touching it. The devices Aaron had placed were well hidden, but Petros was older than circuitry.

He did not look for metal.

He looked for distortion.

He whispered a word in a language that predated language.

The air tightened.

The water in the tank trembled, not violently, but knowingly.

Petros' lips curved.

"Ah."

He turned slowly, robe whispering against stone.

"You hide well," he murmured. "But you forget what I made."

He extended both hands, palms upward.

And began weaving.

Not a summoning.

Not a call.

A tether.

Invisible.

Ancient.

The kind that does not ask permission.

"You no longer will get to choose when you become a dragon," Petros whispered softly. "That decision will be made by me."

He closed his fist.

***

Aaron wasn't sure if his senses were heightened or not, but the classroom smelled like dry-erase markers and recycled air.

He sat three rows from the front, notebook open, pen moving automatically as his history teacher spoke about reconstruction-era legislation.

But right now, he wasn't thinking about American history. His mind was preoccupied with his future.

Then—

His heart skipped a beat.

Just once.

He frowned slightly.

Probably that Coke I just had.

Then it hit again.

Harder.

His chest tightened.

He immediately sat up straighter.

Heat prickled under his skin.

His breath shortened, not from panic.

From ignition.

No.

No, no, no—

Not here.

He gripped the edge of his desk.

The room suddenly felt smaller.

Everything started to sound louder as he could here all of the scattered whispers of his classmates talking underneath the teacher.

His pulse thundered in his ears.

In his ear, Tyler's voice crackled faintly.

"Aaron, something strange came across the feed, I think Petros is about to try something!"

Aaron swallowed.

"I think so too," he muttered through clenched teeth.

The words barely leaving his mouth.

The teacher glanced at him. "Mister Gardon, is everything alright?"

Aaron nodded too quickly.

His veins felt like they were filling with molten glass.

The dragon wasn't rising naturally. It was being pulled.

An external force was calling his feral side to the surface.

His shoulder blades started tingling violently.

His fingers started trembling.

He stood up abruptly.

"Bathroom," he muttered. "Gotta go!"

The teacher barely had time to nod before Aaron was already out the door.

The hallway felt too bright.

Too exposed.

His reflection from the shiny metal lockers flickered, red, just for a split second each time, but still more than he cared for the occurrence.

His pupils narrowed. Not by choice.

Tyler's voice sharpened instantly.

"Aaron. Your vitals are spiking."

"I know," Aaron answered with a growl.

"Are you triggering?"

"I'm being triggered," he replied as his back spasmed.

He then staggered briefly, slamming a hand against the lockers and creating an impossible dent for a student.

A crack formed in the metal beneath his palm.

He clenched his jaw.

Not here...please!

Not in front of everyone.

Heat rolled off him in waves.

The classroom bell rung.

Students started pouring out of the classrooms.

"Aaron?" Tyler's voice rose.

"Petros," Aaron growled under his breath.

"What?"

"He's pulling at my control strings!"

The air shimmered around Aaron's shoulders. A faint outline of wings flickered beneath his jacket.

His heart pounded violently.

He could feel it—

A hook.

Inside his chest.

Dragging upward

***

Somewhere far away—

Petros' eyes were closed.

Sweat beaded at his temples as he maintained the tether.

"Yes," he whispered. "Think you can come into MY HOUSE, and I not know about it? Fight it, oh please fight it!"

He laughed.

***

Aaron staggered into the bathroom and locked the door behind him.

The mirror cracked slightly as he grabbed the sink and countertop, which bent down from his strength.

Scales rippled faintly along his neck, then vanished.

They reappeared.

Then they vanished again.

His breathing came sharp.

Controlled.

"Don't let it take you," Tyler said urgently. "Focus."

"I am focusing," Aaron growled.

"Think about something grounding. Something human."

Aaron squeezed his eyes shut.

His mother's face.

Tyler in the hospital.

The basement monitors glowing in the dark.

Sorrie's voice.

Discipline.

The dragon surged again, as the crowd in the hallway grew silent, the students in their next class.

This time harder.

His vest jacket split slightly along the back line of stitching and his wings started protruding through.

Aaron growled again but swallowed before it became a roar.

"No!" he snarled, not at himself, but at Petros.

***

On the other end of the tether, Petros' smile faltered slightly.

"Interesting," he lamented. "The boy is resisting."

Petros increased the pressure.

***

Aaron dropped to one knee.

The tile beneath him cracked.

Tyler's voice went sharp and calm at the same time.

"You said he feeds on rage."

Aaron nodded faintly.

"Then don't give him rage," said Tyler.

The dragon writhed underneath his skin.

Not wanting to be contained but wanting to be released.

Aaron took a slow, deep breath in.

It was slow, deliberate, and painful.

He then opened his eyes wide.

"You don't control me," he whispered with a growl in his voice.

Fully red, but steady. The hook inside his chest burned and then the tether snapped.

***

In the obsidian chamber, Petros' hand jerked violently backward.

The water in the fish tank exploded outward in a sharp wave, spilling out all the fish and other contents of the tank.

Petros staggered half a step.

He stared at his right palm and noticed the deep burned circle within it.

He smiled slowly.

"Oh, yes you are very strong," he relented. "Taking your head will make me a powerful God indeed!"

***

In the bathroom, Aaron collapsed fully to both knees.

The scales receded fully.

The heat lowered.

The wings retracted into his back.

He stared at himself in the mirror a half a beat as he assessed the damage done to his clothes.

"Vestimentum intaurare," he said calmly and the rips in tears in his clothing all became restored.

He was again fully human.

No signs of his true form in the mirror.

He exhaled once.

Shaking as he stood.

He closed his eyes as he regained control of his heartbeat and respirations.

Tyler's voice came through softly now.

"You still with me bud?"

Aaron nodded, even though Tyler couldn't see him. He then opened his eyes and stared back into his reflection.

"Yeah," he said.

Silence.

Then Tyler added, "he just tested the hell out of you."

163

Aaron ran the sink water and wiped sweat from his face, grabbing a paper towel at the same time.

"And now I know something."

"What?"

Aaron stood slowly.

"He can reach me in order to see me, and where I am."

A beat.

"I can break the reach, but what he can do is enough to locate me."

***

Far away, Petros opened his eyes fully.

"You will not always win that struggle," he murmured to the empty chamber.

He touched the burn mark on his hand.

"And I will come to you, and you will show me your true face," he said angrily.

***

Aaron made it back down the hall to his classroom. He walked in and everyone just stared as he made his way to his seat. "I'm sorry for the interruption," he said as he opened his notebook back up.

"Mister Gardon," started the teacher as Aaron looked up towards him.

"Yes?" he asked.

"The bell rung seven minutes ago," started the teacher as the other students just stared at Aaron if something was wrong with him. "You are now in the wrong class!"

Embarrassed, Aaron looked around the classroom.

He then nodded as he gathered up his things and left out of the class.

23

THE DESERT Heat hit him like a slap, but he felt safer here than in any other place in Arizona.

He texted Sorrie earlier and let her know he would be waiting there, only because he felt safer, or at least the environment would be better than the one his classmates were currently at.

It had been a couple of hours since he was attacked, and he didn't know if he'd have the strength to stave off another.

Suddenly he hunched over and fell to his knees in the sand.

The sky above him bearing witness along with the cacti, tumble weeds, boulders and cliffs.

The tether slammed into him again.

Aaron screamed!

This time there were no lockers.

There were no walls.

There was no hiding.

His spine arched violently as he screamed, with wings tearing out of the back of his jacket as he dug his fingers into the ground, while watching his hands growing and changing without his permission.

His roar tore free, unfiltered.

The dragon surged outward and grew twenty feet upward and sixty feet in width as scales continued erupting fully across his torso.

His jaw elongated as his head once again formed fully with his biological crown in place and FALAP, FALAP, his wings snapped outward instinctively stretched out with a span of one hundred and twenty feet, the mighty beast roared angrily and breathed his blue flame aimlessly towards the sky before staggering upright in full dragon form, eyes blazing, not in control.

He was not a hybrid, and no longer partially a dragon, he was a full dragon, forced to come out by a stronger tether.

Across the desert ridge, a hooded figure stood already waiting.

Sorrie.

When she arrived, she had felt the moment the tether tightened.

Her hoodie flew backwards off her head.

She stepped forward calmly.

"You are bold," she said into the desert air, not talking to Aragon, but to someone else.

Aragons' dragon form convulsed slightly.

His head jerked skyward, then toward her.

His pupils burned.

But there was strain in them.

A second presence began to ripple the air behind him.

The sand shifted.

The horizon darkened, not physically, but energetically.

Petros stepped through like a tear in the world had opened for him.

He did not arrive in fire.

He arrived in certainty.

Wearing an obnoxious ceremonial robe as if he were certain victory would be all but his.

He studied the full dragon before him with quiet hunger.

"There you are," Petros whispered.

Sorrie looked defiantly at him.

"You overreach," she said flatly.

Petros' lips curved faintly.

"You must be the guardian," he laughed. "You did your job well, but now I reclaim what is rightfully mine."

Aragon roared again, but this time it sounded fractured.

Like something inside him was fighting, two directions at once.

Sorrie stepped closer to Aragon, her hood flapping behind her, wind picking up.

"Focus," she commanded sharply.

The dragon's gaze flickered toward her.

Petros extended one hand.

Invisible pressure tightened again.

Aragons' wings twitched violently.

"Do you feel it young one?" Petros asked softly. "The inevitability?"

"You mistake connection for ownership," Sorrie said.

Petros' eyes finally shifted to her.

Cold.

Measured.

"Ah," he said quietly. "You believe this isn't over?"

"I am not his guardian and this is far from over."

"Then why do you stand in front of him?"

Sorrie didn't answer. Instead, she raised her hand outward.

The desert trembled faintly.

The tether flickered.

Aragons' head snapped upward violently.

For a moment, his eyes cleared.

Just slightly.

Petros narrowed his gaze.

"You cannot sever what I've been forging for almost four thousand years," he said.

Sorrie's voice remained calm.

"I don't need to."

She lifted her hand.

"Because he will!"

Aragon roared deeply as Sorrie moved to the far left and out of his way.

Petros' smile vanished.

Aragons' chest heaved.

The dragon inhaled deeply, not to burn.

To stabilize.

The forced control began to level.

The fire in his eyes shifted from wild to focused.

Petros stepped forward one pace.

"Show me," he whispered to Aragon. "Show me your true face."

Aragons' gaze locked onto Petros.

Not enraged.

Not frenzied.

Conscious.

"You don't get it," Aragon growled.

Petros' brow lifted slightly.

Aragon planted his claws into the sand.

Petros attempted to tighten the tether again and Aragon leaned into it instead of fighting away.

Petros' eyes flickered with surprise.

The dragon did not pull back.

He pulled forward.

Using the tether.

Petros staggered half a step as the energy reversed.

Sorrie's lips curved faintly as she smiled.

"Yes," she murmured.

Aragon roared, but this time it was controlled.

Intentional.

The tether snapped violently between them like a breaking chain.

Petros' projection fractured as he stumbled back.

Not destroyed.

But forced backward.

The tear reopened behind him.

He stepped through the tear again, retreating rather than vanishing.

"You've learned quickly," he said angrily.

"And you reveal yourself too easily," Sorrie replied.

Petros' gaze returned to Aragon.

"This is not finished."

"It kind of is," started Aragon, "You just don't know it yet!"

The desert fell silent as Petros dissolved into the tear in fabric.

Aragons' wings trembled once, and then slowly began to retract, inward. His scales receded.

The dragon folded inward as he decreased in size.

He remained collapsed to his knees in human form, breathing hard, but ass naked.

Sorrie approached as he uttered the spell under his breath, "Vestimentum intaurare!"

His clothing reappeared on him and he stood fully up.

"You let him pull you," she said.

"I know."

"And you used it."

Aaron nodded weakly.

"He can force the surface," Aragon said quietly. "But he can't own what's beneath it."

Sorrie studied him.

"For the first time," she said, "you did not fight like prey."

Aragon looked up toward the horizon where his enemy Petros had vanished.

"I'm done being hunted," Aragon said angrily. "The next time he tries that, he dies!"

24

THE BASEMENT LIGHTS were dim except for the monitors.

Tyler sat in a large hoodie, covering the fact he is still bandaged, keyboard before him, eyes sharp.

The spike hit the screen like lightning. It hadn't even been a few hours since the last attack.

"There," Tyler breathed.

His father leaned in. "What in the...."

"That's not anything normal," Tyler said.

The desert feed flickered.

Aaron's vitals surged on the side monitor.

Tyler tapped the mic.

"Aragon. You're spiking. I see you."

***

In the desert, Aragon was airborne again.

Petros had shifted.

Not cloaked.

Not projecting, but fully present and still changing.

His body expanded with grotesque looking limbs elongating, his ribs widening, bone bending outward as if something enormous had been waiting underneath his skin.

Whatever he now was, he grew. He was a towering, massive, non- dragon, non-human, some kind of cross between nightmare and God.

Aragon the dragon roared.

He briefly faltered mid-flight.

Tyler's voice cut in sharply.

"Aragon. we see it, stay with me."

Petros, now a towering beast with jagged limbs and a crown of bone, lunged toward Sorrie.

Aragon didn't think.

He spun mid-air and whipped his tail with surgical force.

CRACK.

The impact slammed Petros sideways and away from her.

Sorrie rolled clear, hoodie torn but body intact.

No injury.

Aragon hovered.

Tyler's voice steady in his ear.

"Good. Good. Keep distance. He's heavier on the right side."

Aragon banked left.

"You see that?" he asked in a rough low growl.

"I see everything," Tyler replied.

Petros roared.

The sound cracked the desert air.

Aragon inhaled.

"I wanna burn him," he said angrily.

"No you don't," started Tyler, remember if you fully give into the rage, you may not be human again."

Aragon steadied.

"No."

He dove instead.
Claws extended.
Controlled.
Not feral.
Yet. He was determined to finish this.

24

THE FIRST NEWS helicopter arrived within minutes.

Then two more.

Then four additional ones, all hardly maintaining good distances.

"THIS IS LIVE FOOTAGE," a reporter shouted into wind. "WE ARE WITNESSING…"

The camera zoomed.

Like watching a movie, a monster and a dragon were tearing through sky.

As the beast clashed, Petros noticed the helicopters and his head snapped quickly in their direction.

His monstrous jaw split open unnaturally and a bright light started to form at his mouth.

Tyler's voice came fast.

"He's targeting the choppers!"

Aragon pivoted instantly.

He surged upward between Petros and the helicopters.

Blue flame erupted from Aragon's mouth, not at Petros, but at the incoming blast.

He intercepted the laser with blue fire which halted the attempted attack.

The helicopter pilot shouted.

"HE JUST SAVED US...THE DRAGON JUST SAVED US!"

FALAP.

FALAP.

Aragon roared, not triumphant, but protective.

FALAP.

Petros snarled and then roared.

"You perform for them now?" he taunted with a deep monstrous tone.

Aragon answered by flying fast towards Petros and ramming him mid-air.

They crash took them to the ground.

No end in sight as the world watched.

***

At Banner Medical Center,

Maya stood frozen before the television mounted in the cafeteria.

A multitude of hospital staff and visitors behind her.

Hands over mouths.

Eyes wide.

The dragon.

Her son, fighting that God awful monster right there on the screen before her eyes.

"You can do it, Aaron," she whispered.

***

Back in the basement, Tyler leaned forward.

"Aragon, listen carefully."

***

Aragon slammed Petros into the ground below.

"I'm listening."

"Remember, you cannot call the sword, Kusanagi, unless you're in full and total control."

Aragon grunted as claws scraped across his chest.

"I know," he said as he grunted.

"No," Tyler said sharply. "I mean fully. If you call it without your dragon side being tamed, she won't answer!"

"I know what the sorceress said Tyler, now please!"

Petros lunged again.

Aragon blocked.

Tyler continued, voice analytical even as chaos roared.

"Also, he can't kill you as a beast."

Aaron paused mid-grapple.

"What?"

"I've been digging more into the recorded myth and lore we saw when this all began. He has to transform into human form," Tyler said quickly. "He needs your head. With a sword. That's why he's trying to tire your dragon form out."

Aragons' pupils narrowed.

Petros smiled mid-attack.

"You learn quickly," Petros hissed.

Aragon understood.

This wasn't just brute force for without reason. He needed the dragon wiped out to make the kill easier.

It was ritual.

And Petros almost played him.

"Thank you, Tyler!" he growled.

26

PETROS FINALLY OVERPOWERED him.

The monstrous form slammed Aragon into stone hard enough to crack it.

The dragon roared loudly.

This time with a feral scream.

Claws tore deep into Petros' monstrous hide.

Wings shredded flesh.

The desert shook.

Petros laughed even as he bled.

"Good," he hissed. "Show me."

Aragon lunged again.

But then, Petros shifted.

The monster started collapsing inward and shrinking.

He stood there as a man.

Calm.

Confident.

He swung his right hand behind his back and his sword materialized with a metallic shimmer.

Ancient.

Waiting.

Aragon descended in full dragon form.

Ready to devour.

The dragon roared

Aragon opened his jaws and then stopped as he slowed mid-air.

He remembered.
He closed his mouth.
FALAP.
FALAP.
FALAP'
FALAP.
He landed with a loud thud as the helicopters hovered above with more distance than when they first arrived.

Petros screamed angrily and moved instantly as he lost control, drawing his sword as he lunged up towards the mighty red dragon.

Blade flashing toward Aragons' neck.

Aragon closed his eyes and released the dragon.

His form quickly collapsed inward.

Scales vanished.

Wings folded into his back as he whispered the spell to call his clothing back into place.

In almost three blinks of an eye, Aragon was human which angered Petros even more.

As the blade came downward, Kusanagi appeared slowly in Aragon's hand.

Not summoned in rage.

Summoned with clarity.

Petros' eyes widened as Aragon blocked his attack.

He then pulled his sword down, stepped forward and impaled his enemy clean through the chest.

Petros gasped.

Aragon twisted the blade free.

Spun once, and with perfect execution, took the head of Petros clean off of his body.

Silence fell across the desert.

The sword, Kusanagi, dissolved from his hand.

Petros, the four thousand plus year old demi-god, dissolved into ashes.

Aragon stood there breathing hard.

Human.

Alive.

And in control. And he walked towards Sorrie as the helicopters landed and as the few news reporters in the area jumped out of their vans and headed towards them.

"You did it Aragon!" Sorrie exclaimed smilingly.

"And I couldn't have done it without you Sorceress," smiled Aragon. "Thank you!"

Sorrie nodded.

"And thank you too Techkick!" he said into the earpiece.

"Yeah, I'm thinking about changing that name," replied Tyler.

Sorrie and Aragon laughed as a thunderous boom from far off in the distance caused the reporters and camera men to stop and look in the direction of the sound.

When they turned around in order to face the young couple hey were running too, they saw immediately that they were gone

27

THE BASEMENT NO longer felt like a war room.

It felt like a game room which had seen something impossible like an ultimate boss defeated.

The monitors were still on, replaying desert footage on mute.

News anchors were trying to explain what they couldn't explain.

But no one was watching anymore, at least not in this household.

They were all there.

The Landons.

Mrs. Landon.

Mr. Landon.

And Tyler.

Mrs. Landon stood near the stairs, surrounded by extension cords and ethernet cables.

She then crossed the room.

No hesitation.

She hugged her son.

Fully.

Firmly.

Tyler froze for half a second, and then smiled, sincerely.

"Yes mom," Tyler said quietly. "Aaron and I are finally safe."

Tyler's father clapped him on the shoulder. "You did good."

Tyler nodded once. "Thanks for helping us."

Tyler sat up his chair, one leg bouncing slightly.

"Thanks for helping me," he said.

Just then, the doorbell rung.

"I'll get that," said Mrs. Landon as she stepped over the multitude of wiring and headed up the basement steps.

From down in the basement, Tyler and his father could hear the commotion at the front door as familiar voices made their way into Tyler's ear canal.

Mrs. Landon soon returned coming down the basement steps with Aaron, Sorrie, and Maya Gardon following her.

"Dude," started Tyler upon seeing Aaron. He got up and they did their customary high five. "You totally kicked his a.."

"Ahem," interrupted Mrs. Landon.

"...butt," said Tyler. "You totally kicked his butt!"

Aaron laughed. "Mr. Landon, this is ..."

"Sorrie," interrupted Sorrie. "Sorrie Cerhess," she said extending her hand.

"Oh Sorrie Cerhess," started Mr. Landon, "When they spoke of you it sounded as if they were saying sorceress."

Sorrie laughed. "Kids," she said smilingly.

Maya tapped Sorrie on the shoulder.

As Sorrie turned around Maya gave her a hug. "Thank you for looking after my son," she said.

"It was my pleasure," started Sorrie, "Your boys are really sweet...Tyler can be a little loud."

"Just like his father," said Mrs. Landon.

"My job is done," started Sorrie. "Aaron...Tyler, I'll be watching you both."

There was a sound at the top of the steps, and everyone looked up. They all then looked again to where Sorrie was standing and she was gone.

"Are we ever not going to fall for that?" asked Tyler.

"Well, it must be hard maintaining a secret life if everyone is always watching her.

"Speaking of which," Mrs. Landon said, looking at Aaron carefully, "if you're going to be... involved in this...hero business"

She gestured vaguely toward the monitors, toward the world.

"...you need to think about a secret identity."

Aaron blinked. "Identity?"

"Yes," she said firmly. "You can't be walking around as yourself if things escalate again, and you have to go full dragon mode. You are going to need a disguise, an alter ego."

Aaron raised an eyebrow.

"You think I need a mask?"

"Yes," she and Maya said at the same time.

Aaron rolled his eyes.

Tyler grinned.

"Actually," Aaron said casually, "I don't."

He stood slowly from the chair.

Everyone watched.

Aaron closed his eyes briefly.

There was no roar.

No wings.

Just a subtle ripple beneath his skin.

When he opened his eyes, the skin around them had shifted.

Not full dragon.

Not full transformation.

But a faint, scaled red pattern formed like a mask across his face, subtle, controlled, stopping just at his cheekbones.

His voice didn't change.

His posture didn't change.

But he was no longer entirely human.

Maya stared.

Mrs. Landon tilted her head slightly, impressed.

Tyler blinked.

"You've been practicing," Tyler said.

Aaron shrugged slightly.

"No, we're still making you a costume," Maya and Mrs. Landon said simultaneously.

Aaron groaned immediately.

Tyler smiled.

"So we're agreed," he said. "Basement stays operational, dragon boy here gets a wardrobe upgrade, and I remain the most important person here."

Aaron shook his head.

"You're impossible."

Tyler smirked.

"And yet," he replied, "indispensable."

Then they all laughed as the basement lights continued to hum softly.

EPILOGUE

NOT MUCH HAD changed over the summer break. Tyler returned to school the next school year, fully healed and with no change to his filter or confidence level.

Signs were now posted over the bathroom doors; *If you see damage anywhere in the bathroom, please report it so repairs can be made.*

Tyler closed his locker and started making his way down the hall when he was pushed backwards. He fell and looked up at his offender as everyone laughed. Tyler remained on the floor for a beat longer than necessary, brushing imaginary dust from his jeans as he looked up at his offender.

Frank, the bully turned around and started waving to everyone to join in on the laughter, "Hey everyone, lets welcome Land-off to senior year!"

As a small number of students laughed, Frank turned to face Tyler when a textbook slammed him in the face, stunning him.

He staggered backward, fell to the floor stunned, clutching his nose.

"Gee that worked better in my head," started Tyler as he took off running. "See ya later Francis!"

"YOU'RE GONNA GET IT LAND OFF!" roared Frank as he and his friends took off after him.

A ripple of confused laughter spread through the onlookers.

***

Tyler flew down the hallway.

He wasn't panicking.

He wasn't scared.

He was excitedly calculating.

He hooked left past the vending machines, ducked into the stairwell, and jumped three steps at a time.

A couple of sophmores flattened themselves against the railing as he passed.

"Sorry!" Tyler called cheerfully.

He hit the basement level and burst through the double doors into the gym.

The echo swallowed his footsteps.

He cut across the edge of the basketball court, sneakers squeaking lightly against polished wood.

Behind him, the stairwell door slammed open.

"GET HIM!"

Tyler glanced back once.

Frank and company charged in, red-faced and determined.

Tyler slowed slightly.

Just slightly.

He smiled.

186

"What are you an idiot Land-off?" asked
Frank. "This is the part where you get your face
pounded!"

"I don't think my fiend back there would like
that.

His friends turned around and started
looking nervous as Frank continued to approach
Tyler with intent to cause bodily harm.

"Whatta you think I'm stupid Land-off? I'm
not gonna fall for the same mistake twice."

As Franks friends took off, a low growl
appeared to be coming from behind him.

Frank slowly turned around and saw a large
red dragon behind him growling.

Frank started shaking nervously and soon
peed himself upon seeing the dragon.

"Boo!" said Aragon causing Frank to start
screaming as he ran out the gymnasium.

Tyler and Aragon started laughing as Aragon
morphed back into his human form.

They pushed through the gym doors into the
afternoon sunlight.

"You're getting pretty good at morphing back
with your clothes already on."

"I had to learn how to mumble the spell as I
morph," said Aaron.

Students moved around them normally.

Cars passed.

Life went on.

Tyler glanced at Aaron.

They gave each other a high five.

"Wanna go grab something to eat?" asked
Tyler.

"Sure," started Aaron, "Mind if we take a quick trip to the desert first? I wanna stretch my wings."

"I'm always down for a trip to the desert," started Tyler. "By the way, I got the keys to your new house!"

About the Author

Derrick J. Truesdale is a healthcare professional who spent over thirty years wanting to tell the stories he believed would both entertain and inspire. Today, those long-held ideas have become interconnected science fiction and fantasy novels that stand alone while forming a larger, evolving universe.

His worlds can be dark at times—but they are never without purpose. He writes with the hope of encouraging others to explore their imagination, embrace transformation, and discover strength in unexpected places.

Welcome to the world of Semaj, where seemingly separate stories share deeper connections waiting to be discovered

www.SemajBooks.com.